Simple Chess

Simple Chess

Michael Stean

Faber and Faber

LONDON & BOSTON

First published in 1978
by Faber and Faber Limited
3 Queen Square London WC1
Phototypeset in V.I.P. Times by
Western Printing Services Ltd, Bristol
Printed in Great Britain by
Redwood Burn Ltd, Trowbridge and Esher

British Library Cataloguing in Publication Data
Stean, Michael
  Simple chess.
  1. Chess – Handbooks, manuals, etc.
  I. Title
  794.1'2   GV1445

  ISBN 0–571–11215–3
  ISBN 0–571–11257–9 Pbk

Contents

1. Introduction

Don't be deceived by the title—chess is not a simple game—such a claim would be misleading to say the least—but that does not mean that we must bear the full brunt of its difficulty. When faced with any problem too large to cope with as a single entity, common sense tells us to break it down into smaller fragments of manageable proportions. For example, the arithmetical problem of dividing one number by another is not one that can in general be solved in one step, but primary school taught us to find the answer by a series of simple division processes (namely long division). So how can we break down the 'problem' of playing chess?

Give two of the uninitiated a chessboard, a set of chessmen, a list of rules and a lot of time, and you may well observe the following process: the brighter of the two will quickly understand the idea of checkmate and win some games by P–K4, B–B4, Q–R5 and Q×KBP mate. When the less observant of our brethren learns how to defend his KB2 square in time, the games will grow longer and it will gradually occur to the players that the side with more pieces will generally *per se* be able to force an eventual checkmate. This is the first important 'reduction' in the problem of playing chess—the numerically superior force will win. So now our two novices will no longer look to construct direct mates, these threats are too easy to parry, but will begin to learn the tricks of the trade for winning material (forks, skewers, pins, etc.), confident that this smaller objective is sufficient. Time passes and each player becomes sufficiently competent not to shed material without reason. Now they begin to realise the importance of developing quickly and harmoniously and of castling the king into safety.

So what next? Where are their new objectives? How can the problem be further reduced? If each player is capable of quick development, castling and of not blundering any pieces away, what is there to separate the two sides? This is the starting-point of *Simple Chess*. It tries to reduce the problem still further by recommending various positional goals which you can work towards, other things (i.e. material, development, security of king position) being equal. Just as our two fictitious friends discovered that the one with more pieces can expect to win if he avoids any mating traps, *Simple Chess* will provide him with some equally elementary objectives which if attained should eventually decide the game in his favour, subject to the strengthened proviso that he neither allows any mating tricks, nor loses any material *en route*.

Essentially, *Simple Chess* aims to give you some of the basic ideas for forming a long-term campaign. It also shows you how to recognise and accumulate small, sometimes almost insignificant-looking advantages which may well have little or no short-term effect, but are *permanent* features of the position. As the game progresses, the cumulative effect begins to make itself felt more and more, leading eventually to more tangible gains. This style of play is simple and economical both in its conception and execution. Combinations and attacks are shelved for their proper time and place as the culmination of an overall strategy. Given the right kind of position it is not so difficult to overwhelm the opposition with an avalanche of sacrifices. The real problem is how to obtain such positions. This is the objective of *Simple Chess*.

Undoubtedly the best way to improve your chess is by studying master and grandmaster games. For this reason I have used a selection of such games as a medium through which to put across the fundamental principles of simple chess. These games are mostly not of the type to capture the limelight of chess literature because they are too simple and unsensational, but for this very reason they are suitable for showing off clearly the basic ideas I want to convey.

As a preliminary to splitting the elements of simple chess into an array of recognisable objectives, as will occur in the ensuing chapters, I want to give you something of the flavour of what is to come in the form of three introductory games containing most of the concepts and strategies to be elaborated later on. The first is a victory by ex-World Champion Mikhail Botvinnik over the Hungarian International Master Szilagyi in Amsterdam, 1966. One of the truly great masters of strategy, Botvinnik gives a typically powerful and very instructive display. We pick up the play in diagram 1 with Botvinnik (White) to move:

The position may at first sight seem quite good for Black. His pieces occupy good squares in the centre, his king is very safe and he has a lead in development having already connected his rooks on the back rank while White is a long way from doing so. However, positionally he has problems arising from the exchange of his queen's bishop for a knight. In the long run he will find difficulty in defending his white squares. We shall see what this means in more tangible terms as the game progresses.

12 P–QN4

A space-gaining move. The centre is fixed and White does not want to advance on the kingside for fear of exposing his own monarch, so the logical zone for expansion is on the queenside.

12 ... B–N3

13 P–QR4 KR–Q1

Black dare not hit back with 13 . . . P–QR4 because of 14 B–R3 followed by N–B4 or N–N3 with lots of dangerous possibilities on the QR3–KB8 diagonal.

14 Q–B2 QR–B1

Black already finds himself lacking a good plan. A better idea was 14 . . . N–B1 followed by N–K3 and P–QR4 trying to get a grip on QB4 or Q5. Black's difficulties stem from the fact that he has no good outpost for his pieces.

15 B–K2

In contrast Botvinnik's advance has given him a nice square on QB4 which he can occupy with either a knight or a bishop.

15 ...   P–B4??

Two question marks for a move which does not actually lose any material may seem a bit harsh, but I want to emphasise the point that before 15 . . . P–B4 Black merely had problems, but now he is lost.

16   P–N5!

2

Why is Black lost? Material is equal and White hasn't got a piece beyond the second rank. The answer lies in the pawns. White has two beautiful squares on QB4 and Q5 plus a mobile pawn roller on the left flank, whereas Black's pawns constrict his own pieces terribly, particularly the bishop. Botvinnik now treats us to a vigorous exhibition of technical chess as he converts these advantages into a win.

16   ...   N–K1
17   N–B4   N–Q3
18   B–N5!

A surprise tactical shot, but its aims are positional.

18   ...   P–B3

The point of the combination. Black is forced to weaken yet another white square (K3) in the heart of his position. Refusal to fall in with White's plans is even more unpalatable:
  (i)   18 . . . Q×B 19 N×N R–N1 20 B–B4.
  (ii)   18 . . . N–B3 19 N–K3 followed by N–Q5.

19   B–K3   N×N

20	B×N+	K–R1
21	P–R5	B–B2
22	KR–Q1	N–B1

An exchange of rooks will not heal Black's wounds. On the other hand, neither will anything else.

23	Q–R2	R×R+
24	R×R	R–Q1
25	R×R	B×R
26	P–R6	

Conquering yet another white square (QB6) and simultaneously releasing the queen from her defence of the QRP in preparation for more active service.

26	...	P–QN3
27	K–N2	

White's control of the position is so great that he could inscribe his initials on the board with his king if he wanted. Being rather less self-indulgent, Botvinnik contents himself with one preparatory king move before embarking on the winning process. On general principles, his king will feel safer on a white square.

27	...	Q–Q2
28	Q–K2	N–N3
29	B–N3	

At last an attack, but there's no need for any excitement. The outcome is a mere formality. With a bishop having the mobility of a tortoise with rheumatism, Black is in no position to offer any real resistance.

29	...	N–K2
30	Q–B4	P–R3
31	Q–B7!	K–R2

31 ...Q×P loses a piece to 32 Q–B8+ K–R2 33 Q×B Q×B 34 Q×N.

32	B–B4	Q–Q3
33	P–R4	

Botvinnik now weaves a mating net on the white squares.

33	...	Q–Q8
34	Q–K8	

With the threat of B–B7–N6 mating. There's no defence.

34	...	P–B4

35 P×P   N×P
36 B–N8+ K–R1
37 B–B7+ and mates next move.

A perfect illustration of what is known as a *white square strategy*, something we will explore in more depth later on. For the moment, however, I merely want to draw your attention to the effortless simplicity with which Botvinnik established and drove home his advantage. With the possible exception of 18 B–N5!, none of his moves could in any way be described as surprising or difficult to visualise. They were all really rather obvious. So why cannot everybody play like that? Well, they can providing they recognise and understand the importance of *structure*. The most important single feature of a chess position is the activity of the pieces. This is absolutely fundamental in all phases of the game (opening, middlegame and *especially* endgame), a theme which I hope will become increasingly apparent as the book progresses. The primary constraint on a piece's activity is the pawn structure. Just as a building is constructed around a framework of iron girders, a chess game is built around an underlying structure of pawns. The difference lies in the fact that the iron framework is fixed, whereas the chessplayer has a certain amount of flexibility with his pawns.

The job of the chessplayer must therefore be to use his skill to create a pawn set-up which will allow his own pieces the optimum freedom and stability, while denying his opponent's similar scope. This is the problem of *structure*, which will be dealt with in some depth.

3

To take an example, let us go back to the position of diagram 2 and examine it from a structural point of view. Removing the pieces from the board, but leaving the pawns, we have diagram 3. From this we see very clearly why White's position is structurally superior. He has two very strong squares or *outposts* for his pieces on QB4 and Q5. They are strong because neither can be challenged by a black pawn. In contrast, Black has no outposts at all. So arithmetically speaking White had a 2–0 lead in outposts, a very healthy state of affairs. Bearing this in mind, notice the vital role played by the white PQB3 in guarding Black's natural outpost on Q5. If White were ever to play the positionally abysmal P–QB4? he would not only give Black his long awaited outpost, but would also smother his own QB4 square, thus equalising the outpost score to 1–1 at a stroke. Moreover the damage would be irreversible. Pawns cannot move backwards. If you inadvertently put a piece on a bad square, you can always retract it at the cost of some time (and face), but in the case of a pawn you are lumbered with it for the rest of the game. Think twice about pawn moves, especially in the centre.

4

Returning to diagram 3, is there any way for Black to improve matters, structurally speaking? Certainly. If he could advance P–QB5, the world would suddenly be a much happier place for him. Look at diagram 4. Black now has three excellent squares QB4, Q6, QN6, while White has to be content with one (Q5). So we see that White's QB4 square is strategically the focal point of the position. Just as the outcome of a real battle may depend on control of a high point or mountain dominating the surrounding terrain, a chess game can hinge around the struggle for control of one key square. In this case it is White's QB4. Do you recall Botvinnik's 15th move B–K2? It may not have seemed terribly significant at the time, but it in fact shows that he had already fully recognised the strategic importance of the QB4 square. Clever fellows these Russians!

We now turn our attention to an even more striking demonstration of the power and importance of structure, this time given by the great master of defence Tigran Petrosian. The ninth game of his Candidates' Match with Lajos Portisch (Black) started 1 N–KB3 N–KB3 2 P–QB4 P–KN3 3 P–QN3 B–N2 4 B–N2 P–B4 5 P–N3 P–Q3 6 B–N2 P–K4 7 0–0 N–B3 8 N–B3 0–0 9 P–Q3 N–KR4 10 N–Q2 B–N5 11 P–QR3 B–R3 reaching the position of diagram 5.

5

At a glance the black pieces may seem to be menacingly poised for a kingside attack. On the other hand a quick look at the pawn structure reveals that White has an excellent outpost on Q5, but how does that help? It certainly has no immediate value, as 12 N–Q5 N–Q5! 13 B×N KP×B would allow Black to develop a lot of pressure on the king's file. However, the Q5 square is there to stay and if it cannot be profitably utilised at present, it is nevertheless a good investment for the future. With this in mind Petrosian chose

12 P–QN4!

The classical way to exploit a structural advantage in the centre is with a thrust on the flank, but here accurate calculation is also required. In the event of 12 ...P×P 13 P×P N×QNP White plays 14 B–QR3! (but not 14 B×P N×QP!) with three possibilities:

    (i) 14 ...N×QP? 15 P–KR3 now wins a piece.

    (ii) 14 ...N–QB3 15 N(Q2)–K4 winning the PQ6.

    (iii) 14 ...P–QR4 15 R–N1 regaining the pawn with advantage as N×QP still fails to P–KR3.

One might reasonably ask if it was not simpler to drive away Black's bishop with 12 P–KR3 before playing P–QN4 so as to avoid all the above complications based on the pin on White's king's pawn. The answer is that White does not want to make any pawn move in front of his own king until is is *absolutely necessary*, as it merely provides Black with a ready-made target to attack. For instance, 12 P–KR3 B–Q2 13 P–QN4 P–B4 and P–B5 could well be dangerous for White.

| 12 | ... | N–Q5 |

Black has some very dangerous threats. Not only is 13 ...B×N and 14 ...N–N6 winning the exchange on the cards, but the Tal-like sacrifice 13 ...N–B5! 14 P×N B×P followed by Q–R5 is also in the air.

| 13 | P–R3! | |

A sense of timing is the key to good defensive play. Here Petrosian accepts the weakening of his kingside pawns as he realises that he can thereby completely repulse the attack.

| 13 | ... | B–K3 |
| 14 | P–K3 | P×P |

An anti-positional capture, but he has no alternative. After 14 ...N–QB3 15 P×P P×P 16 N–N3 Q–K2 17 N–R4 he simply loses a pawn for nothing.

15	P×P	N–QB3
16	P–N5	N–K2
17	B×P	

Another well-calculated little venture which increases White's positional advantage still further.

| 17 | ... | B×RP |
| 18 | B×R | B×R |

18 ...Q×B 19 Q–B3 is very much the same as the game

| 19 | K×B | Q×B |

20 Q–B3!

A very strong move, if an equally obvious one. After 20 ...Q×Q 21 N×Q not only is Black structurally quite lost, but he has not even enough time to defend his QRP in view of the threatened P–N4–N5 winning a piece.

20 ...   Q–N1

This leads to the immediate and rather quaint loss of a piece, but there is nothing better to recommend. If you are wondering why Black is so abjectly lost, compare the pawn structures.

21 P–N4   N–N2
22 Q–B6!

Very neat. The double threat of Q×N and Q–R4! is decisive. After the further moves 22 ...N(N2)–B4 23 P×N N×P 24 P–K4 N–N2 25 K–K1 N–R4 26 Q–R4 P–B4 27 N–Q5 Black resigned.

A resoundingly decisive game to win against a World Championship contender, but Petrosian didn't have to work all that hard. His pawns in their own quiet way did all the work for him.

In both of the preceding games Black's structural deficiency has taken the form of weak squares rather than the pawns themselves being weak. In most cases these two effects (weak squares, weak pawns) go hand in hand, as we shall see. For the moment, here is a game in which White uses the presence of weak pawns in the enemy camp to tie down the black pieces and so launch a mating attack, despite the absence of queens.

6   Adorjan-Mukhin, Luhacovice 1973
1 P–K4 P–K4 2 N–KB3 N–QB3 3 B–N5 P–QR3 4 B×N QP×B 5 0–0 P–B3 6 P–Q4 B–KN5 7 P×P Q×Q 8 R×Q P×P 9 R–Q3 B–Q3 10 QN–Q2 N–B3 11 N–B4 B×N 12 P×B 0–0–0

The position is tense. Black's pawn on K4 is weak, but that is his only weakness. The doubled QBP's are not weak, not yet at any rate. On the other hand White's doubled pawns could well become weak as they are on an open file. Moreover, Black has an outpost on KB5 and if given time for N–R4 and KR–B1 could easily seize the advantage, so . . .

13 B–N5

Immobilising the knight and threatening QR–Q1, which wins a pawn.

13 . . .   P–QN4

The only way to meet the threat of 14 QR–Q1. The life expectancy of Black's KP would not be increased by 13 . . .P–KR3 14 B–R4 with B–N3 in prospect.

14 N–R5   P–QB4
15 P–QB4!

Fixing the Black QBP on a vulnerable square before it marches on to the safety of B5.

15 . . .   QR–B1

He needs to unpin the knight. 15 . . .P–N5 would allow White to start an attack on the QR file with 16 P–QR3, while 15 . . .P×P? 16 N×P is contrary to all Black's aims.

16 P×P

In general terms White does not want to lift the blockade of the QBP, but here he has a particularly incisive follow-up.

16 . . .   P×P
17 P–QR4!

The point. White recaptures control of the vital QB4 square by force, for if now 17 . . .P–B5 then simply 18 R(Q3)–Q1 and the pawn on B5 cannot be held.

17 . . .   P×P

This lets the white rooks loose, but 17 . . .P–N5 18 N–B4 N–K1 is also dreadful for Black. It is no accident that White's conquest of the QB4 square is rapidly followed by the collapse of Black's game.

18 N–B4   N–K1
19 R×P

Black's tortuous manoeuvres (the rook has moved to enable the knight to retreat to defend the bishop which defends his pawns!) have maintained material equality, but left his king out in the cold.

A typical example of the necessity to defend weaknesses drawing the defending forces out of position.

19 ...   K–N2

What else?

20 P–B4!

The attack begins in earnest. If now 20 ...P×P, then 21 P–K5 R–B4! 22 B×P! B–K2 (22 ...R×B 23 N×B+) 23 N–R5+ gets to grips with the black king.

20 ...   P–R3
21 P×P   P×B
22 P×B   P×P

Or 22 ...N×P 23 R–N3+ K–B1 (23 ...K–B3 24 N–K5 mate) 24 N–K5 winning.

23 R–N3+ K–B1
24 R–R7

Black is helpless against the threat of R(N)–N7 followed by N–N6+ mating. His pieces are mere spectators.

24 ...   P–Q4
25 P×P   Resigns.

The moral behind this trilogy of games should be clear: Look after your pawns and your pieces will look after themselves. To 'look after' one's pawns is not the most difficult thing in the world, and the next few chapters illustrate how this can be done and how the pieces can be made to co-operate with their pawns.

2. Outposts

We all like to attack. There is a streak of sadism running through every chessplayer that helps him to sit back contentedly sipping a cup of tea while his opponent, head in hands, tries frantically to avert mate in three. But where do attacks come from? The mere action of pushing one or two pieces in the general direction of the enemy king does not constitute an attack. In general a successful attack can only be launched from a position of strength in the centre of the board. This 'position of strength' can take various forms, the simplest being an outpost.

As the name suggests, an outpost is a square at the forefront of your position which you can readily support and from where you can control or contest squares in the heart of the enemy camp. To be useful an outpost must be firmly under control and so should ideally be protected by a pawn. Conversely your opponent should not be given the opportunity to deny you access to your outpost, so in particular it must be *immune to attack by enemy pawns*.

This last condition is far and away the most important and can indeed almost be taken as the defining property of an outpost.

7

So as not to blur the issue with too many words let us look at some examples of outposts purely in terms of pawn structure. In diagram 7 there are plenty to be seen. White, from a structural point of view, has outposts on Q5, QN6, QN4, KN4. One might also regard QB4 and QR4 as outposts, for although they are not supported by pawns, they certainly are immune from attack by them. Black has supported outposts on KB5, KN6 and unsupported ones on KN4 and KR4. You may have noticed that all of White's outposts are on the queenside, Black's on the kingside, so with such a pawn structure one would normally expect to see White attacking on the left flank, and Black on the right.

This is all very theoretical and hypothetical, far from the stark realism of practice. For example, one rarely encounters the plethora of outposts seen in diagram 7. You often have to be satisfied with one, or less!

8 Tal-Bronstein, 26th Soviet Championship
Tiflis 1959
1 P–K4 P–K4 2 N–KB3 N–QB3 3 B–N5 P–QR3 4 B–R4 N–KB3 5 0–0 B–K2 6 R–K1 P–QN4 7 B–N3 P–Q3 8 P–B3 0–0 9 P–KR3 N–QR4 10 B–B2 P–B4 11 P–Q4 N–B3 12 QN–Q2 Q–N3 13 P×BP P×P.

A quick look at the pawn structure reveals that White has one outpost (on Q5), Black has none. However, life is not quite so simple, as White is not the master of his QB4 square, so Black can at any time create an outpost on Q6 by P–QB5. A typical state of affairs in these Ruy Lopez positions.

14 N–B1

This knight is the obvious candidate for residence on Q5, and so heads for the jumping-off square K3, from where it incidentally also eyes the KB5 square.

14 ... B–K3
15 N–K3 QR–Q1
16 Q–K2 P–N3

9

For the moment Bronstein has everything under control. White's outpost on Q5 is well covered and his knight has also been denied the KB5 square. So what is there for White to do? The answer must be to harass the defenders of the Q5 square.

17 N–N5 P–B5!

Black quite rightly refuses to be bullied into retreating his bishop. He fully realises the importance of White's outpost on Q5, and so is willing to allow his pawns to be shattered by 18 N×B P×N in order to take it away from him for ever.

18 P–QR4

Unable to make any further headway in the centre, Tal creates a diversion on the wing. In doing so he slightly weakens his own queenside (Black now has an outpost on QN6), but this is acceptable as the latent power of his Q5 outpost prevents Black from undertaking anything active on the queenside. If, for example, Black tries the natural 18 ...N–Q2, heading for B4 and his own outposts on Q6 and N6, White's game suddenly springs to life with 18 P×P P×P 19 N–Q5!

18 ... K–N2

A useful move, improving his king position and waiting for White to show his hand.

19 P×P P×P
20 R–N1

Preparing to challenge Black's queenside supremacy with P–QN3. The dissolution of Black's QBP would destroy his outposts before his pieces ever got near them.

White's manoeuvres on the queenside are not so much aimed at improving his own position as at eroding his opponent's—a sort of sabotage campaign.

20   ...   N–QR4

To discourage P–QN3.

21   N–B3!

A good time to admit that his knight is serving no useful purpose on N5. As already pointed out, there is no future in taking the bishop as Black recaptures with the pawn and White's proud outpost is no more.

21   ...   Q–B2
22   N–Q5!

10

The moment we've all been waiting for, not to mention the white queen, rook and bishop who have been patiently queuing up behind the KP for some time. White's decision to play his trump card now is prompted by the fact that Black's knight has been drawn out of play to QR4. This may not seem to be very significant, but with the rapid opening up of the position which must surely follow, the absence of even a single piece from the central field of battle will cause great difficulties for Black.

22   ...   B×N

The alternative 22 ...N×N 23 P×N B×P 24 N×P gives White a dangerous attack as he not only threatens to win a pawn with 25 N×NP, but also to launch a direct assault on the black king with 25 N–N4 or 25 Q–K3. A good example of an attack arising naturally from a 'position of strength in the centre', the position of strength in this case being the Q5 square.

23 P×B   KR–K1

A flexible move. He wants to see which way White will take the KP before deciding how to capture the QP.

24 Q×KP Q×Q
25 N×Q   N×P
26 R–R1

White's position is beginning to flow very smoothly.

26 ...   N–N6
27 B×N   P×B
28 B–R6+!

11

A stunning blow. If 28 ...K×B, then 29 N×P+ K–N2 30 N×R R×N 31 R–R5 and Black is under great pressure. In the endgame an active rook and a pawn often outweigh bishop and knight, particularly so in this case as Black's queenside pawns are very vulnerable, e.g. 31 ...R–QN1 32 R–K5 B–Q1 33 R–R3! (33 R–R7+ N–B2 may hold) picking off a second pawn.

Notice the tremendous energy which has been released from the white position by 22 N–Q5!

28 ...   K–N1

Plagued by time trouble, Bronstein tries to play safe and runs into worse trouble. Grim though it may be, he must take the bishop.

29 N–B6   R–QB1
30 QR–Q1 R×N
31 R×N

There is no defence to the double threat of R×B and R×P. The game concluded 31 ...P–B3 32 R×P P–N4 33 R×P K–B2 34 R–N7 R–K3 35 R×R K×R 36 P–R4 R–KN1 37 P–B4 B–B4+ 38 K–B1 P×RP 39 R–N5 R–QB1 40 P–B5+ K–Q3 41 P–QN4 P–R6 42 R×B P–R7 43 B–B4+ Resigns.

An instructive and exciting display of outpost play.

Particularly noteworthy was the terrible restraining influence exerted on Black by the continual 'threat' of N–Q5. Having completed his development very harmoniously, Black found it extremely difficult to undertake any active plan without allowing the inevitable N–Q5. Indeed, he only had to decentralise one piece (20 ...N–QR4) and the white knight jumped down his throat.

We have just seen how an attack can spring from a central outpost. More obviously, an outpost in the vicinity of the enemy king is an excellent platform from which an offensive can be launched.

12 Benko-Najdorf, Los Angeles 1963
1 P–Q4 N–KB3 2 P–QB4 P–QB4 3 P–Q5 P–Q3 4 N–QB3 P–KN3 5 P–K4 B–N2 6 B–K2 0–0 7 N–B3 P–K4 8 B–N5 P–KR3 9 B–R4 P–KN4 10 B–N3 N–R4 11 P–KR4 N–B5 12 P×P P×P 13 B–B1 B–N5 14 Q–B2.

Black has mishandled the opening. True, he has firmly established his knight on KB5, but in doing so he has also given White an outpost on KB5. An eye for an eye you might well say, but White's eye is dangerously near the black king while the white king still has the right of abdication to the queenside.

14 ...   B×N?

A further misconception. Black needs this bishop to have any chance of contesting his KB4 square.

15 P×B   N–Q2

16 O–O–O

With the disappearance of the white king, Black's impressive-looking outpost on B5 bears little relevance to the position compared to White's. The one thing White must avoid is taking the knight, as Black would gleefully recapture with the king pawn thereby releasing his bishop and giving himself outposts on K4 and Q5.

16 ...   R–K1

Preparing to defend his kingside with N–B1.

17 B–R3!

13

Bound for B5. If the bishop is not taken, White can simply close his eyes and play B–B5, R–R2, QR–R1, N–Q1–K3. When he opens them again, he is sure to find a win fairly quickly.

17	...	N×B
18	R×N	N–B1
19	QR–R1	N–N3
20	N–Q1	R–QB1
21	N–K3	R–B2
22	N–B5	R–KB1
23	Q–Q1	P–B3

Black is condemned to total passivity, whereas White can manoeuvre almost *ad infinitum* for an opening. Such positions are invariably lost for the defender in the long run, but here White immediately produces a neat and incisive finale.

24 P–B4!

14

24 ... KP×P
25 Q–R5! N–K4

If 24 . . . P×B, then 25 Q×N and there is no way to avoid R–R8 mate, while 24 . . . K–B2 25 Q–R7 R–N1 26 N–R6+ also wins out of hand.

26 Q–R7+

Black resigns on account of 26 . . . K–B2 27 Q×B+ K–K1 28 Q×R+ K×Q 29 R–R8+ and 30 R×Q.

In most cases outposts, or potential outposts, are clearly apparent from the pawn structure, but occasionally a keen strategical eye is needed to realise the importance of a certain square. The Lord gave Botvinnik two very keen strategical eyes.

15 Botvinnik–Donner, Holland 1963
1 P–QB4 N–KB3 **2** N–KB3 P–K3 **3** P–KN3 P–Q4 **4** B–N2 B–K2 **5** 0–0 0–0 **6** P–N3 P–QN3 **7** B–N2 B–N2 **8** P×P N×P **9** P–Q4 P–QB4 **10** P×P B×P **11** QN–Q2 N–Q2 **12** P–QR3 N(Q4)–B3 **13** P–QN4 B–K2.

The centre of the board appears to be a demilitarised zone and there is certainly no sign of any outposts. White's next move adds a new dimension to the position.

14 N–Q4!

> Sensing that QB6 can be made into an effective outpost for the knight, as he can support it with P–N5.

14 ... B×B

> If he tries to cover his B3 square with 14 ...N–Q4, then White replies 15 P–K4 N(4)–B3 (15 ...N–B2 16 R–B1 secures the vital square) 16 P–K5 N–Q4 17 N–B4 and White suddenly has an outpost on Q6.

15 K×B Q–B2

16 Q–N3 KR–B1

> The right rook to put on QB1, as he may later want to challenge a white pawn on N5 by P–QR3.

17 KR–B1 Q–N2+

18 Q–B3!

> An exchange of queens would suit White very nicely—18 ...Q×Q+ 19 N(2)×Q followed by N–B6, R–B2 and R(1)–B1 with a complete stranglehold on the game.
>
> If White can ever establish his knight on B6, the black rooks will be suffocated.

18 ... N–Q4!

> A clever defensive manoeuvre designed to defend the QB3 square by blocking the long diagonal.

19 P–K4 N(Q4)–B3

20 P–N5

16

The struggle is reaching a critical point. Botvinnik has completed his preparations for N–B6, so the question arises: can Black engineer enough exchanges to nullify the smothering effect of N–B6? Let us look at some tries:

(i) 20 ...R×R 21 R×R R–QB1 22 N–B6! B–B4 (or B1) is precisely the kind of thing Black is trying to avoid. White can follow up with 23 N–B4 and 24 R–Q1, the advanced knight rendering Black helpless against the build-up on the queen file.

(ii) 20 ...N–K4(!) 21 Q–K2 R×R 23 R×R R–B1 24 R×R Q×R 25 P–B4 N(K4)–Q2 26 N–B6 B–B1, when grabbing a pawn with 27 N×P would be reckless on account of the reply 27 ...Q–B7! Instead 27 N–B4 maintains White's initiative, but the total exchange of rooks had eased the defence a little.

In the game, Donner tries a different approach which involves exchanging all the rooks on the QR file, but is surprised by White's 25th move.

20	...	P–QR3
21	N–B6	B–B1
22	P–QR4	P×P
23	P×P	R×R
24	R×R	R–R1

17

25 R–Q1!

A deep move. Botvinnik realises that his opponent can do little on the QR file (25 ...R–R7 26 Q–N3 or even 26 N–B4) and that he needs a pair of rooks on the board to make full use of his outpost.

25 ...   N–K1

A symptom of White's pressure. His queenside advance has left Black with an outpost on QB4, but the immediate occupation with 25 ...N–B4 loses a pawn after 26 B×N.

26	N–B4	N–B4
27	P–K5	

Unveiling some deadly tactical possibilities on the long diagonal, which leave Black in virtual zugzwang, viz.

(i) 27 ...N–B2 28 R–Q7! N×R 29 N–K7+! winning the queen.

(ii) 27 ...N–R5 28 N–K7+! Q×N 29 Q×R.

(iii) 27 ...R–R5 28 R–Q8 R×N 29 R×N with the deadly threat of N–K7+.

(iv) 27 ...K–R1 (to cut out the N–K7+ possibilities) 28 N×P! Q×N(N3) 29 Q×P and the bishop is lost (29 ...N–B2 30 R–Q8!).

You may wonder why all these combinations are suddenly bouncing into the picture. The answer is that combinational possibilities almost invariably accompany an overwhelming positional superiority, such as the one White has here.

27	...	R–B1
28	R–R1	

Wins! The threat is R–R7 winning the queen, and 28 ...R–R1 loses to R×R and N–K7+, a familiar theme.

| 28 | ... | R–B2 |

Or 28 ...Q–B2 29 R–R7 N–N2 30 B–Q4 B–B4 31 B×B P×B 32 N(B6)–R5.

29	R–R7	Q×R
30	N×Q	R×N
31	N×P	Resigns.

Thus far we have seen how an outpost can act as a pivot about which the game swings to and fro. Rather like the trunk of a tree, an outpost is a central pillar from which branches of attack grow naturally. You only have to be careful that you do not choose a branch that breaks off as you crawl along it. Fine, but what happens when you sit at the board and find that you have no outpost? You can build one.

18 Fischer–Gadia, Mar del Plata 1960
1 P–K4 P–QB4 **2** N–KB3 P–Q3 **3** P–Q4 P×P **4** N×P N–KB3 **5** N–QB3 P–QR3 **6** B–QB4 P–K3 **7** B–N3 P–QN4 **8** 0–0 B–N2 **9** P–B4 N–B3 **10** N×N B×N.

White has no outposts and his king pawn is hanging, but he does have a lead in development. If he tries to utilise this by blindly hacking his way through the centre with 11 P–K5? he will not be impressed with the result after 11 ...P×P 12 P×P B–B4+ 13 K–R1 Q×Q 14 R×Q N–N5. A bit more subtlety is required—he needs an outpost, so ...

10 P–B5! P–K4

Giving way without a fight. Less obliging is 10 ...Q–Q2, though after 11 P×P P×P 12 Q–Q4! B–K2 13 B–N5 White has an enduring initiative, if no outpost as yet.

Black's most interesting move here is 10 ...P–N5 trying to drive the knight well away from Q5 before conceding the square, i.e. 10 ...P–N5 11 N–R4 P–K4! and White's outpost is of little use to him as he cannot occupy it. This idea would work very well for Black were it not that he is mauled by the piece sacrifice 10 ...P–N5 11 P×P! P×N 12 P×Pch. K–K2 (12 ...K–Q2 13 P–K5) 13 Q–K1! Some sample lines:

(i) 13 ...P×P 14 B×P (threatening P–K5) N×P 15 R–B4 P–Q4 16 R×N+! P×R 17 B–R3+ with a savage attack.

(ii) 13 ...Q–N3+ 14 B–K3 Q–N2 15 P–K5! P×P 16 Q×P etc.

(iii) 13 ...Q–B2 14 Q×P N×P 15 Q–R3 and Black has terrible problems.

I give these lines to illustrate the role played by White's development advantage. It is not in itself sufficient to force home a mating attack, but it does force Black to make positional concessions (conceding the Q5 square) in order to avoid meeting a grisly end. Attacking play and positional play are not incompatible opposites. On the contrary, they go hand in hand.

12 Q–Q3

His positional goal (an outpost) attained, White must return to more mundane affairs, namely the defence of his king pawn.

12 ...   B–K2
13 B–N5!

When an outpost has been set up the next and most logical thing to do is to chase off, exchange or harass defending pieces which cover the square in question. Here White takes the opportunity to trade his black-squared bishop (which can itself never directly control Q5) for the enemy knight which does control Q5, thereby making his outpost an absolutely permanent feature of the position. Black could and probably should have prevented this with 12 ...P–KR3.

13 ...   Q–N3+
14 K–R1   0–0
15 B×N

All according to plan.

15 ...   B×B
16 B–Q5!

Beautifully simple. The last defender of Q5 is eliminated.

16 ...   QR–B1
17 B×B   R×B
18 QR–Q1

The final preparation for N–Q5 which if played at once could be met by 18 ...Q–Q5! 19 Q×Q P×Q and Black has good chances to save the endgame as the white KP and QBP are rather weak.

18 ...   KR–B1
19 N–Q5   Q–Q1
20 P–B3

'This is the kind of position I get in my dreams' was Fischer's comment on reaching a position similar to this one as White in a skittles game against the late Russian Grandmaster Leonid Stein. Fischer then proceeded to prove that even he is human by losing it. In fact, the position Fischer remarked upon was much less favourable for White than this one. Here the white knight seemingly dominates the whole board and is completely unassailable. Black cannot exchange it off for anything less than a rook, but can undertake nothing while the tyrannical beast rules.

20 ...   B–K2
21 R–R1!

What bridge players might term as a safety play. White can virtually win this position as he pleases, but Fischer characteristically chooses the line of minimum risk. His plan is simply to play P–QR4 and Black's queenside pawns will prove to be indefensible.

A more adventurous, but less scientific, approach would be 21 P–B6 B×P 22 R×B!? P×R 23 R–KB1 with a strong attack.

21 ...   P–B3

This loses, but so does everything else, e.g. 21 ...B–B1 22 P–QR4 P×P (22 ...R–N1 23 N–N4 R(B3)–N3 24 P–R5 R(3)–N2 25 N–B6) 23 R×P and the QRP soon falls.

22 P–QR4 R–N1?

Black is losing a pawn at least, but evidently not one to do things by halves, he gives away a rook instead.

23 N×B+ Resigns, on account of 23 ...Q×N 24 Q–Q5+.

26 Outposts

We have so far seen illustrations of how to set up, secure and exploit outposts, but no clue has been given as to how to play *against* an outpost. The most usual way to counter an enemy outpost is to cover it with as many pieces as possible so that when he occupies it with a piece you can capture enough times to force him eventually to recapture with a pawn.

20

For example, in diagram 20 White has an outpost on K5, but N–K5 can always be met by N×N and after recapturing with the pawn his outpost is gone. Clearly he needs to bring another minor piece to bear on K5, so White to move would play 1 B–KN5 and follow up with B–R4–N3. If on the other hand Black is on the move he would seek to prevent this. 1 ...P–KR3 is the obvious way, but a more active solution is preferable—namely 1 ...Q–K1 (so as to meet 2 B–KN5 with 2 ...Q–R4! threatening R×N) or 1 ...Q–N3. Either move gives Black a fine position.

21

If you are unable to cover your opponent's outpost, then extremely active harassing tactics are needed. Diagram 21 shows a marked structural resemblance to diagram 19, but the position features a vital difference—the white knight has not yet reached Q5. Indeed it is at least four moves away. This gives Black some breathing space, which he must make good use of. If the knight reaches Q5 he is lost.

The diagrammed position occurred in the game Unzicker–Fischer, Varna 1962. Fischer continued:

| 1 | ... | R–R5! |

Immobilising the knight (2 N–Q2? R–Q5).

| 2 | P–B3 | Q–R3 |

Not falling into the trap 2 ...KR–R1? 3 Q×R+!

| 3 | P–R3? | |

Relieving the non-existent back rank threats. He should play 3 QR–Q1 threatening N–B1–Q3–N4.

3	...	R–B1
4	KR–K1	P–R3
5	K–R2	

White is playing planlessly. He may have been intending 5 R×R P×R 6 N–B1, but 6 ...P–R6 sees Black breaking through on the queenside.

| 5 | ... | B–N4 |

Black's position is looking very good.

| 6 | P–N3? | Q–R2 |
| 7 | K–N2 | R–R7! |

With the double threat of R×P+ and R×BP. Surprisingly there's no defence.

| 8 | K–B1 | R×BP! |

Resigns, as after 9 R×R (9 P×R Q–B7 mate) R–B6+ 10 K–K2 R–B7+ 11 K–Q1 Q×R his position is wrecked. The poor knight never even moved!

The lesson to be learned here is that structure alone is not quite everything. The pieces must be able to co-ordinate with the pawn structure. After all, what use is a body without a soul?

3. Weak pawns

In the previous chapter we looked at pawn structure from the point of view of outposts and how an outpost acts as a pivot, about which the pieces can swing into action. Without such an outpost as foundation, pieces tend to lack the stability necessary for a successful assault and are liable to be driven back in confusion. It is sheer folly to try to attack directly a well co-ordinated and developed position. Many players underestimate the defensive resources inherent in such positions and will in game after game bash their heads against a brick wall instead of using their heads to first weaken the cement. The point they repeatedly fail to appreciate is that a very definite superiority in force is needed to ensure that an attack will be successful. This superiority can take either one of two forms:

(i) Better development. This is simply a case of superiority in numbers, the aggressor being able to feed more pieces into the attack than the defender has available to fight them off.

(ii) Better co-ordination. This is a much more subtle form of advantage which one must work hard to build up. The idea is to disarm the defence by first tying its pieces down to the defence of certain points, so that when the storm does break they have very little scope or opportunity to react.

Here we concern ourselves primarily with the second condition. Outposts provide the necessary stability for the attacker, but something must also be done to destroy the defender's co-ordination. This is where the second aspect of pawn structure, weak pawns, comes in. If the defending forces can be reduced to the menial task of protecting pawns, they will not be able to offer much opposition to a full-scale offensive.

So what exactly is a weak pawn and how is it recognisable? The answer is both simple and logical. A weak pawn is one which cannot be protected by another pawn and so requires support from its own pieces. Note that the criterion is the *ability* to be protected by another pawn, not the existence of such protection. Take the example of two adjacent pawns on, say, Q4 and K4. Neither protects the other but each has the ability to be guarded by the other, by advancing. We must therefore say that the weakness or strength of two adjacent pawns depends on whether or not they are able to advance if the necessity arises.

Diagram 22 gives us an example of adjacent pawns (Q3, QB3) which are very definitely weak, because neither can move. P–Q4 is never feasible, as it leaves the KP in the soup after the reply P×P (note for this purpose the power of the white rook on K1), while P–QB4 leaves Black riddled with holes. The continuation of the game Hecht–Forintos illustrates well the combination of outpost play (KB5) and the exploitation of weak pawns.

1 B–N5

A simple developing move which exerts great pressure on the black pawns. White has many threats to win a pawn, including the spectacular 2 N×KP!

1 ... KR–Q1

Black has no choice but to defend passively. If he tries to iron out his weaknesses with 1 ...B×B 2 N×B P–Q4, he merely tees himself up for the knock-out punch, viz. 3 Q–R5 P–KR3, and now White can win spectacularly by 4 N×P+ P×N 5 Q×P KR–K1 (forced) 6 R–K3! with a winning attack for the piece, or settle for the methodical 4 N×B Q×N 5 Q×N! Q×Q 6 N–K7+ K–R2 7 N×Q K×N 8 P×P winning a pawn.

Although White cannot hope to achieve success by a direct kingside attack, Black's frantic attempts to cover up his weaknesses could well set something up for him.

2 R–QB1

Turning the focus of attention to the QBP (he threatens to win it by capturing twice on K7), while preserving the harmony of the white position.

2 ... QR–B1

3   R–B3!

A multi-purpose move illustrating clearly the maleffects of weak pawns. White creates options to double on the QB file (with Q–B2), double on the Q file (R–Q3) or possibly transfer the rook to KN3 at some later date. Black has no opportunity to reciprocate, but must on every move be prepared to meet each contingency. We see a definite rift between the mobility of the two armies opening up. When the gap becomes wide enough White will be able to bludgeon his way through the black position without encountering much resistance.

3	...	B×B
4	N×B	N–B5
5	P–N3	B–R4

If 5 ...N–K3, 6 Q–N4 is extremely unpleasant for Black.

6	Q–Q2	N–K3
7	N×N	Q×N
8	Q–N5!	

Suddenly it's all over. There are three distinct threats (Q×Pmate, Q×B, N–K7+) and no defence to all of them.

The speed of capitulation should make it abundantly clear that pieces tied to the defence of weak pawns are often unable to defend themselves.

The most common form of pawn weakness encountered in practical play is the isolated pawn—one which has lost its neighbours and stands alone in face of the enemy. Such a pawn has two basic deficiencies: firstly it requires defence, and secondly the squares immediately in front of it make ideal outposts for the other player. To see in more tangible terms what this means, let us look at a famous game Fischer won on his road to the World Championship against an ex-World Champion Tigran Petrosian.

White: Fischer   Black: Petrosian

1	P–K4	P–QB4
2	N–KB3	P–K3
3	P–Q4	P×P
4	N×P	P–QR3
5	B–Q3	N–QB3
6	N×N	NP×N
7	0–0	P–Q4
8	P–QB4	

23

Black has built up a very solid-looking pawn centre, but only at the cost of neglecting his development. Fischer uses the time he has gained, not to launch any violent offensive (Black's position is quite solid enough to absorb anything like that), but to break up the black centre before its pieces have the chance to support it. A pawn centre must be adequately supported by pieces to be effective, else it merely becomes a target of attack.

8 ... N–B3

Under no circumstances can Black consider capturing away from Q4, as this would leave him with 'split' pawns on QR3, QB3 whose weakness would plague him for the rest of the game. A plausible alternative was 8 ...P–Q5, trying to keep the centre closed, but yet another non-developing move must be regarded with some suspicion.

9 BP×P BP×P
10 P×P P×P

Ideally Black would prefer to recapture with the knight, but after the reply 11 B–K4! he would in the long run be unable to avoid the isolation of his pawn owing to the pin on the diagonal.

Having successfully saddled Black with two isolated pawns, Fischer now gives us a perfect lesson in how to go about taking full advantage of them.

11 N–B3 B–K2
12 Q–R4+!

A deep move. Given time to castle, play B–N2 and P–Q5, Black would be very happy. Remember, weak pawns are only a handicap if they result in the pieces being driven to bad or passive

squares in order to defend them. Now however, 12 ...B–Q2 13
Q–Q4 gives the white queen a dominating view of the world while
leaving the black pieces hemmed in behind the QP. Rather than
submit to this, Petrosian sets a cunning trap.

12 ...   Q–Q2!?
13 R–K1!

Fischer does not allow his vision to be blurred by a lust for
materialism. He could win the exchange by 13 B–QN5 P×B 14
Q×R, but after 14 ...0–0 ...B–N2 and ...P–Q5 Black's whole
position suddenly springs to life and White finds himself in
trouble. Always be wary of grabbing material at the cost of the
co-ordination of your pieces.

13 ...   Q×Q
14 N×Q   B–K3
15 B–K3   0–0

24

A convenient time to stop and reassess the situation. The
exchange of queens has helped White somewhat, in that without
queens less can happen to interrupt or obscure the basic flow
of the game. Nevertheless White's overall strategy remains
unchanged. He must use the weakness of the two isolated pawns
to tie down the black pieces while maximising the activity of his
own.

16 B–QB5

One of the secrets of endgame play is to realise which pieces to
exchange, which to retain. Here White wants to trade off the
black-squared bishops for two reasons:

    (i) As the weak pawns stand on white squares, the black

squared bishop is the only piece which *cannot* be tied down to their defence.

(ii) White wants to use the QB5 square as an outpost for his knight.

16	...	KR–K1
17	B×B	R×B
18	P–QN4	

The next logical step in the chain. Having just traded the 'right' pair of bishops, he does not want the black pawns to run away onto black squares, for in that case he will have traded the wrong bishops! Now White can always meet ...P–QR4 with P–N5 and the massive passed pawn must prove decisive. This process of fixing weaknesses on squares where they are most readily assailable is particularly common and should always be borne in mind when playing against weak pawns.

It is also worth noting that P–QN4 establishes the outpost on B5. Whether you approach the position from the point of view of outposts or weaknesses, the move 18 P–QN4! cries out to be played.

18	...	K–B1

In endgames the king is a very powerful piece and should be used as such. The immediate value of this move is to unpin the bishop, but in the longer term Black would like to bring his king to Q3 from where it would probably cement his position together.

19	N–QB5 B–B1
20	P–B3

White also needs to use his king. Despite the fact that each of his pieces is more actively placed than its opposite number there is no immediate way to break through, so the king must be used to increase the pressure.

Mistaken would be 20 R×R? K×R 21 R–K1+ K–Q3, when Black can probably hold the position. It is important not to allow the black king across the king's file. Once on the queenside it can to some extent release the pieces from their task of defending pawns for more active service.

20 ...   R(K2)–R2

A very curious move, but its motivation is worth closer study. There are no points in the white position to counter-attack, so Black must seek some method of 'improving' his own position. The obvious try is to bring the king to Q3, but the only available route K–K1–Q1–B2–Q3 is both long and hazardous. The other possibility is to transfer the bishop to a more active defensive post. At the moment the bishop effectively defends the QRP, but plays no further part in the game, other than interfering with the rooks' co-ordination and generally getting in the way.

It could fulfil its duties much more efficiently from QN4, but the problem is how to get there. The normal try would be 20 ...N–Q2 21 N–N3 (exchanges help the defence) N–K4 22 B–B1 B–Q2 intending B–N4 on the next turn. At this point however the weakness of the QP takes its toll, for after 23 KR–Q1 (not 23 QR–Q1 B–N4 24 R×P? N×P+!) Black must abandon his plan in order to save the pawn. Petrosian's move has the same idea (B–Q2–N4) in mind.

21 R–K5   B–Q2

According to plan.

22 N×B+

A slightly surprising decision in that one would not normally want to trade such a dominating knight for a struggling bishop, but here the exchange enables Fischer to penetrate with his rooks. It is really a question of trading one advantage (superior minor piece) for another (superior rooks).

22 ...   R×N

23　R–QB1　R–Q3

> To try to free the other rook from the defence of the QRP.

24　R–B7　N–Q2
25　R–K2　P–N3

> Black has been totally starved of constructive moves. Let us examine the position in detail to see why:
>
> (a) If the knight moves, there comes R(2)–K7 winning.
>
> (b) King moves also allow R–K7.
>
> (c) If Black tried to trade off his passive rook with 25 ...R–K1, White could complete the tying-up process by 26 R×R+ K×R 27 R–R7 N–N1 28 P–N5! (There are other ways to win, but this is the neatest) 28 ...P×P 29 B×P+ K–B1 (29 ...N–Q2 leads to a lost K+P endgame after 30 K–B2 K–Q1 31 B×N R×B 32 R×R+ K×R 33 K–K3 K–Q3 34 K–Q4 etc.) 30 R–N7! R–Q1 31 K–B2 and Black has no moves at all. White simply blockades the QP with his king and queens the QRP.
>
> (d) Obviously the rook on Q3 cannot move.
>
> (e) 25 ...P–QR4 26 B–N5 N moves 27 R(2)–K7 etc.
>
> The necessity to guard two isolated pawns has reduced Black to pawn moves alone. White now only has to add one more weight, namely his king, and the scales must tip.

26　K–B2　P–KR4
27　P–B4

> With the idea K–N3–R4–N5 and P–B5.

27　...　P–R5
28　K–B3　P–B4
29　K–K3

> The king has been denied an entrance on the kingside, but the chessboard is a big place. There is plenty of room on the other side.

29　...　P–Q5+

> Naturally K–Q4 must be prevented.

30　K–Q2　N–N3

> Rather than wait for the king to ooze in, Petrosian makes a final bid for some counterplay. Purely passive defence would lose to, *inter alia*, the plan of B–B4, K–Q3 and R–K6.

31　R(2)–K7　N–Q4

32　R–B7+　K–K1

33 R–QN7 N×BP
34 B–B4! Black resigns.

26

A quaint final position which shows the immense power of even a small co-ordinated force. Despite having a pawn more, Black is quite helpless in face of the threat of R–KN7–KN8. E.g. 34 ...P–N4 35 R–N7 R–B3 (35 ...N–N3 37 B–B7+) 36 R–KN8+ R–B1 37 B–B7+.

A truly classic game, one worth continual restudy. It shows with perfect simplicity all the steps necessary to transform a superior pawn structure into a win. The one underlying theme running through the whole game is the way the black pieces are systematically deprived of all mobility.

27

Next we look at doubled pawns, a subject littered with common misconceptions. Contrary to popular belief, doubled pawns are not invariably weak but in many cases are definitely advantageous. Naturally doubled *isolated* pawns are to be avoided, but there is no reason to fear having doubled pawns when no isolation of pawns occurs.

For example, in the following line of the Vienna Opening 1 P–K4 P–K4 2 N–QB3 N–KB3 3 B–B4 N–B3 4 P–Q3 B–N5 5 N–B3 P–Q3 6 0–0 B×N 7 P×B N–QR4 8 B–N3 N×B 9 RP×N 0–0 10 P–B4 (diagram 27), the only effect of the doubled pawns is to give White a small but unquestionable advantage. Why? Basically because White has more central pawns than his opponent (he leads by two QBP's to one). In the opening and middlegame centre pawns are more valuable than flank pawns. Moreover the white pawns provide a very effective barrier against the enemy bishop without in any way impeding their own bishop. Above all there is no question of White having any weak pawns—they all protect each other, except for the 'base' at QB2 which is completely unassailable. There is of course very little wrong with the Black position either, but the Danish Grandmaster Bent Larsen has been able to turn White's slender advantage into a win. It requires infinite patience and perfect technique, but it is possible.

The pros and cons of doubled pawns may be thought of in terms of a military line along which forces are evenly distributed. One can reinforce a certain part of the line only at the cost of weakening another. Naturally the value of the policy depends on how serious the weakening effect is. To translate this notion into chess terms, consider the pawn complex K3, KB3, KB2, KR2. The pawn tripleton K3, KB3, KB2 is by itself quite strong as it controls a lot of central squares without exhibiting much to attack. The weakness lies with the isolated KRP and the squares in front of it. Returning to the context of our analogy we can say that the centre has been strengthened at the cost of weakening the flank. If the latter effect turns out to be inconsequential then the doubling of the pawns must be reckoned to be a good thing.

Aaron Nimzovitch was maybe one of the first to have a deep understanding of doubled pawns. A great chess thinker and experimentalist, he pioneered what is nowadays generally considered to be the 'perfect' defence to 1 P–Q4, namely 1 ...N–KB3 2 P–Q4 P–K3 3 N–QB3 B–N5—the Nimzo-Indian. Black's basic strategy is to take the knight at the right moment, doubling the White's QBPs and then try to prove that they are weak. Naturally this idea has received many ramifications over the years, but it still can be made to work even at the highest levels.

White: B. Spassky   Black: R. J. Fischer
5th Match Game, Reykjavik 1972

1	P–Q4	N–KB3
2	P–QB4	P–K3
3	N–QB3	B–N5
4	N–B3	P–B4
5	P–K3	N–B3
6	B–Q3	B×N+
7	P×B	P–Q3

Having traded off his bishop to double the pawns, Black must be careful to contain the enemy QB. This he does by setting up his central pawns on *black* squares to reduce the bishop's scope.

8	P–K4	P–K4
9	P–Q5	N–K2
10	N–R4	

Preparing to open lines for his bishops with P–KB4. He can meet 10 ...N–N3 with 11 N–B5.

10	...	P–KR3
11	P–B4	N–N3!

Black is himself willing to accept doubled pawns to open lines for his pieces. In a few moves we shall see exactly why.

12	N×N	P×N
13	P×P?!	

This helps Black. Better is to keep the tension with 13 0–0.

13	...	P×P
14	B–K3	P–N3
15	0–0	0–0
16	P–QR4	P–QR4!

28

Black has given himself a backward QNP, an isolated KP and doubled KNPs. Why? to keep the position blocked. The white bishops are badly hemmed in by their own pawns and without prospect of ever breaking out. We have here a new source of 'weakness'. White's pawns are bad not so much because they require defence, but simply because they get in the way. In some sense one can think of them being weak because the pieces cannot avoid defending them.

17	R–N1	B–Q2
18	R–N2	R–N1
19	QR–KB2	Q–K2
20	B–B2	

White has already run out of constructive ideas. Although his pieces are all very well placed, they have no effect because they cannot co-operate with the pawns. The game has already been reduced to a question of whether Black can create enough threats to win. White can only wait.

20	...	P–KN4
21	B–Q2	Q–K1
22	B–K1	Q–N3
23	Q–Q3	N–R4

The first attempt to make progress. Black's knight heads for a semi-outpost on B5. I use the term semi-outpost because White can defend that point with a pawn (P–KN3), but does not want to unless absolutely necessary because it leaves a hole for Black's bishop on R6 in dangerous proximity to the king.

24	R×R+	R×R
25	R×R+	K×R
26	B–Q1	N–B5
27	Q–B2??	

29

An outright blunder losing immediately. He must play 27 Q–N1 when the White position is bad, but difficult to crack. However the psychological effect of having to hold a prospectless position for what might seem to be an infinite amount of time does nothing to aid the defender's concentration.

27 ...   B×P!

White resigns. After 28 Q×B Q×KP he loses everything. A game decided by pawns, not pieces.

Of course one cannot play the Nimzo-Indian with the *idée fixe* of doubling White's QBPs at all costs. An auxiliary strategy is needed, as White can always decide not to accept doubled pawns if he so wishes.

White: S. J. Hutchings   Black: R. D. Keene
Woolacombe 1973

1 P–QB4 N–KB3
2 N–QB3 P–QN3
3 N–B3   B–N2
4 P–Q4   P–K3
5 P–KN3 B–N5

White is a little confused by Black's unusual move order (2 ...P–QN3) and has allowed transposition into a Nimzo-Indian in which he is committed to fianchettoing his KB. The kingside fianchetto is not altogether desirable against the Nimzo, as the white pawn on QB4 lacks support with the KB on KN2.

6 B–Q2

Opting to avoid the doubled pawns, but only at the cost of some time.

6 ...   P–QB4

Plan B. Black utilises the time he has gained to switch to an attack on White's centre, using the power of the fianchettoed QB.

7 P–QR3

Although this simultaneously acquires the two bishops and succeeds in defending the centre, it also represents a further loss of time. Less ambitious but safer was 7 P×P and 8 B–N2.

7 ...   B×N
8 B×B   N–K5!

Back to plan A. The prospect of doubled QBPs is just as unpalatable as before, so White is tempted to waste still more time to avoid being saddled with them.

9   Q–B2   N×B
10   Q×N   Q–B3

 30

There is something vaguely symphonic about the course of this game. We are given the first subject (threat to double QBPs), second subject (attack on Q4), then the first again and now we have both of them together! The threat is B×N winning a pawn and White dare not capture away from Q4 because of the doubled pawns he would have to endure after Q×Q+.

11   R–Q1   B×N!

A fine move that tells us much about doubled pawns. Black is not doubling White's KBPs in order to attack them, but to create an outpost for his knight on Q5. The quartet of pawns KB2, KB3, KN3, KR2 in itself forms a very strong pawn complex, but the metamorphosis of White's KP into a KBP means that he can no longer control his Q4 square. We can see exactly the same idea in a game Karpov-Browne, San Antonio 1972, which opened 1 P–QB4 P–QB4 2 P–QN3!? N–KB3 3 B–N2 P–KN3?! 4 B×N! P×B 5 N–QB3 and White has a beautiful outpost on Q5. Recall the analogy with the military line. The effect here of doubling the pawns is to strengthen the flank, but weaken the centre.

12   Q×B

Still determined to avoid the dreaded doubled QBPs. Understandably so, as after the alternative 12 P×B N–B3 13 P–Q5 Q×Q+ 14 P×Q N–R4 his pawn structure does have a very unkempt appearance.

12	...	Q×Q
13	P×Q	N–B3
14	P×P?	

But this is a serious mistake. Admittedly 14 P–Q5 N–Q5 is good
for Black because of his powerful knight, but it at least does not
offer him any obvious point of attack. The text move however
opens the QN file and so leaves White with a *backward* QNP open
to attack along the file. The fact that it opens the Q-file for White
is irrelevant here as the black king comfortably thwarts any aspirations he might have in that direction.

14	...	P×P
15	B–N2	R–QN1
16	R–Q2	R–N6!

31

Displaying the second feature of a backward pawn on an open file,
namely that the square in front of it makes a splendid outpost.
With an advanced outpost for his rook, one for his knight, and a
backward pawn to attack Black has, positionally speaking, everything he could ever ask for.

17 K–Q1

White's only hope is to try and hold the QN file with his king.
Incidentally, his last move sets a little trap. Black can apparently
now pick up a pawn with 17 ...N–K4. Indeed so, but after 18
K–B2 N×P (either) 19 K×R N×R+ 20 K–B3! White picks up a
knight.

17	...	K–K2
18	P–B4	N–Q5

19 K–B1   P–KR4!?

Black is also capable of setting traps, but this one is much more subtle. The automatic choice of move here is 19 ...KR–QN1, but first he creates a diversion. We shall presently see why.

20 P–KR4

Why not prevent P–R5? It can't do any harm, can it?

20 ...   KR–QN1
21 B–B1

The penny drops. Black was threatening to pull off the *coup* 21 ...R×KNP!! 22 P×R N–N6+ 23 K–Q1 N×R 24 K×N R×P+ and R×B. To set this combination up he had to lure the KRP away from KR2, so that ...R×KNP could not be recaptured with the RP, in which case he would be unable to pick up the bishop at the end.

21 ...   R–KB6

Decisive infiltration. The threat is simply N–N6+.

22 K–Q1   R×RP!

Another elegant blow (23 P×R R–N8 mate) and indeed the last one, as White resigned at this juncture to avoid any further humiliation.

In recent times there has been a trend to go to almost any lengths in order to weaken enemy pawns, especially to inflict doubled isolated pawns. The first victim of this trend was the previously much revered fianchettoed KB. For example:
1 P–QB4 P–KN3 2 N–QB3 B–N2 3 N–B3 P–QB4 4 P–Q4 P×P 5 N×P N–QB3 6 N–B2 B×N+! (The classical chess theorist might advocate exchanging this piece for nothing less than a rook!) 7 P×B N–B3 followed by getting to work on the pawns with P–Q3, B–K3, R–QB1, N–K4 (or QR4) etc. A double-edged idea as Black's kingside is severely weakened by the loss of its bishop, but one that seems to work well enough in practice.

Similarly Petrosian's idea in the English opening: 1 P–QB4 N–KB3 2 N–QB3 P–KN3 3 P–KN3 P–Q4 4 P×P N×P 5 B–N2 N–N3 6 P–Q3! (Delaying the development of his KN so that he can give up his bishop for the black knight when it comes out of hiding) 6 ...B–N2 7 B–K3 N–B3 8 B×N+! P×B 9 Q–B1.

Even the rook is sometimes called upon to lay down its life to split up some pawns. For example, in the following well-known line of the Dragon Sicilian 1 P–K4 P–QB4 2 N–KB3 P–Q3 3 P–Q4 P×P 4 N×P N–KB3 5 N–QB3 P–KN3 6 B–K3 B–N2 7 P–B3 N–B3 8 Q–Q2 0–0 9 B–QB4 B–Q2 10 P–KR4 P–KR4 11 0–0–0 R–B1 12 B–N3 N–K4 13 B–R6, Black nonchalantly continues 13 ...B×B 14 Q×B R×N! 15 P×R Q–B2 with a perfectly good game despite having a whole exchange less.

To conclude this section we look at a complex struggle between a World Champion and ex-World Champion which highlights the tendency of weak pawns always to have the last word, even when there seems to be some counterplay about.

White: A. Karpov   Black: B. Spassky
Spartakiad 1975

1	P–Q4	N–KB3
2	P–QB4	P–K3
3	N–KB3	P–QN3
4	P–KN3	B–N2
5	B–N2	B–K2
6	N–B3	0–0
7	Q–B2	P–Q4

Black must challenge the centre before P–K4 comes. The alternative 7 ...P–B4 is less good as White can counter with the following ingenious manoeuvre: 8 P–Q5 P×P 9 N–KN5! (White wants to recapture on Q5 a piece so as to make an outpost there) 9 ...N–B3 10 N×QP P–N3 11 Q–Q2! and White stands better because of his outpost on Q5. Playing the black side of this in his match against Korchnoi, Karpov continued 11 ...N×N 12 B×N R–N1? overlooking the winning combination 13 N×RP! (the knight cannot be taken because of 14 Q–R6+ K–N1 15 Q×P+ K–R1 16 Q–R6+ K–N1 17 B–K4 P–B4 18 B–Q5+ R–B2 19 Q–N6+).

8	P×P	N×P
9	0–0	N–Q2
10	N×N	

A well-timed exchange, as 10 ...B×N 11 P–K4 B–N2 12 R–Q1 gives White an impressive centre. Consequently Black decides after all to block his bishop by recapturing with the pawn.

10	...	P×N
11	R–Q1	

Anticipating the freeing move ...P–QB4, Karpov envisages that the black pawn on Q4 may well become weak. There is at the moment no compulsion for Black to break out with P–QB4, but he will find it difficult to avoid for ever.

| 11 | ... | N–B3 |
| 12 | N–K5 | |

Now however White threatens to establish an outpost on QB6, so Black has little choice in the matter.

| 12 | ... | P–B4 |
| 13 | P×P | B×P |

Spassky avoids the so-called 'hanging pawns' which would result from 13 ...P×P. Generally speaking hanging pawns are strong so long as they can be maintained together (i.e. on QB4, Q4), but if one is forced to advance, the rear one becomes very weak. Here White would be immediately able to break up the hanging pawns (after 13 ...P×P) by 14 P–K4 P–Q5 15 N–B4 obtaining an outpost for the knight. On the other hand, the isolated pawn Black now acquires is an obvious target, moreover a stationary one on account of the pin on the long diagonal.

| 14 | N–Q3 | B–Q3 |
| 15 | B–B4 | |

We have seen before (cf. Fischer–Petrosian) this idea of exchanging Black's active bishop, leaving only the passive defender on the board.

15	...	R–K1
16	P–K3	N–K5
17	B×B	Q×B

46 Weak pawns

18 N–B4

A very good square for the knight. The pressure on Black's QP is obvious, but he is not without some counterchances based on his own well-placed knight.

18 ...   QR–B1
19 Q–R4   Q–K2

With the sacrificial possibility ...N×KBP in mind. Black must resort to tactical sorcery to keep his game alive.

20 Q×P

33

A bold decision requiring very delicate calculation, but a correct one.

20 ...   N×BP!

If he tries to preface this sacrifice with 20 ...P–Q5 to open the diagonal, there comes 21 P×P N×KBP 22 R–K1! and Black is left with hanging pieces, an undesirable alternative to hanging pawns.

21 N×P!

21 K×N would lose to 21 ...Q×P+ 22 K–B1 R–B7.

21 ...   B×N
22 Q×Q   N×R!

The best chance. After 22 ...R×Q 23 R×B White has a winning endgame, not so much in view of his extra pawn which is rather sick but because of his 2–1 pawn majority on the queenside and his powerful bishop.

23 R–B1!

Prettily exploiting the back rank weakness to get his last piece into play with tempo. The quaint point is that this move is only possible because of the knight on Q1 which prevents the rook being taken with check.

23 ...   R–N1
24 Q–N4   B×B
25 K×B   N×P+
26 K–N1

And White eventually converted his material advantage into a win: 26 ...R–K3 27 Q–KB4 R–Q1 28 Q–Q4 R(1)–K1 29 Q–Q7 N–N5 30 R–B8 N–B3 31 R×R+R×R 32 Q–N7 R–K3 33 Q–N8+ N–K1 34 P–QR4 P–N3 35 P–QN4 K–N2 36 Q–N7 P–R4 37 K–N2 K–B3 38 P–R3 R–Q3 39 P–R5 P×P 40 P×P R–K3 41 P–R6 N–B2 42 P–R7 R–K2 43 Q–B6+ K–K4 44 K–B3 Resigns.

4. Open files

'Put your rooks on open files' is a piece of advice every beginner receives, and a very sound piece of advice it is. But like all pieces of sound advice, it can prove to be inadequate, or worse.

34

Look at diagram 34. An innocent-looking position, but if Black (to move) dutifully seizes the only open file with 1 ...QR–Q1 he quickly runs into trouble after 2 B–K3:

(i) 2 ...P–QR3 3 B–N6 R–Q2 4 KR–Q1 R(K)–K2 (or 4 ...R(Q)–K2 5 B–Q8! R–K3 6 R–Q7 with decisive penetration) 5 B–B5 R×R 6 R×R and the white rook reaches the seventh rank (6 ...R–B2? 7 R–Q8+ K–R2 8 B–Q6 wins the rook!).

(ii) 2 ...P–N3 (to prevent the bishop driving Black off the Q file) 3 P–R5! P–QB4 (forced) 4 P×P P×P 5 R–R7 followed by KR–R1 with a winning position, e.g. 5 ...:R–R1 6 KR–R1 R×R 7 R×R R–K3 8 R–N7 and K–N3–B4–N5 mopping up the queenside pawns.

Why the storm from a clear sky? Because files do not always operate on the first come, first served system. If you look back at variation (i) you will see that Black ran into trouble on the Q file, despite having first option on it. So where did he go wrong? Firstly he failed to appreciate the disparity in strength between the bishops. The white bishop was able in variation (i) to drive the black rooks off the Q file single-handed, and in variation (ii) enabled White to open the QR file for his own rooks. In both cases the black bishop was a spectator. And secondly Black had no reason to occupy the Q file anyway. Occupation of an open file is of no value, unless there is a chance of penetration. Here the white king prevents any possible insurgence on the Q file. In particular the entry square on the seventh rank, invariably the most important, is also guarded by the white bishop, making the Q file an entirely prospectless avenue for Black. If the black king were on, say, K3 rather than N1, the Q file would be just as worthless for White.

Returning to the diagram, the correct treatment by Black is 1 ...K–R2!, preparing to trade off White's dangerous bishop, and after 2 R–Q1 (threatening of course R–Q7) 2 ...KR–Q1 (Not 2 ...QR–Q1? 3 B–K3 gaining a tempo by the attack on the pawn) 3 B–K3 B–R3!, because the pawn-grabbing attempt 4 R×R R×R 5 B×P allows Black in on the seventh rank (5 ...R–Q7+). Better is 4 B–B5 threatening to seize control of the file with B–K7, but Black can defend with 4 ...B–N4 to be followed by bringing his king across to K3. It must be stressed that open files only have value as a means of feeding rooks (or possible queens) into the enemy position, so that a file has no value unless there is somewhere along it an entry point, i.e. an advanced point on which a rook can safely land. The ideal entry point is on the seventh rank (i.e. Q7 on the Q file, etc.). Every rook secretly dreams of landing on the seventh, making a ninety-degree right (or left) turn and eating its way through the enemy lines. There is something magical about the number seven for a rook. Alternatively points of entry on the eighth, sixth or even fifth rank can be just as effective. But there must be one, otherwise the file is useless. In this respect the king can play an important role. In the endgame, there is no piece better equipped to defend entry points than the king. For example a king on K2 simultaneously covers three entry squares on the Q file (Q1, Q2 and Q3, or Q8, Q7 and Q6 from the opponent's point of view), a feat which no other piece (apart from the queen of course) can perform. This makes the location of the opposing king a vital factor in assessing the value of an open file in the endgame. The basic rule is the further from the king, the better. Returning to our example, we see that the Q file was not a useful commodity for Black because of the proximity of the white king, yet the very same file was potentially lethal in White's hands as the black king was far away.

We can see this principle operating in the following variation of the Sicilian Defence, the so-called Maroczy Bind: 1 P–K4 P–QB4 2 N–KB3 N–QB3 3 P–Q4 P×P 4 N×P P–KN3 5 P–QB4 N–B3 6 N–QB3 N×N 7 Q×N P–Q3 8 B–K3 B–N2 9 P–B3 0–0 10 Q–Q2 B–K3 11 R–B1 Q–R4 12 N–Q5 Q×Q+ 13 K×Q.

35

Theory assesses this position as very favourable for White. Why? Because the QB file is going to be opened and the white king is much closer than the black one. As a result White is able to take control.

13   ...   B×N

There is no choice but to take the knight, and 13 ...N×N 14 BP×N B–Q2 15 R–B7 is immediately decisive, so the text move is forced.

14   BP×B   KR–B1

Everything seems O.K. with Black, as 15 R×R+ R×R 16 B×P achieves nothing in view of 16 ...R–R1 regaining the pawn at once, but the favourable position of the white king presents him with other possibilities.

15   R×R+   R×R

16   P–KN3!

36

The key move. White intends to drive the enemy rook off the file with B–R3. He is only able to employ this strategy of conceding the open file then playing to regain it, because the black rook has no point of entry.

Let us analyse the position a little to see just how serious the threat of B–R3 can be:

(i) 16 ...K–B1 (bringing the king across to bolster the queen-side) 17 B–R3 R–B5 18 P–N3 R–B2 19 B×P. White has won a pawn for nothing (19 ...B–R3+ 20 K–Q3).

(ii) 16 ...P–QR3 (to keep the pawn out of harm's way) 17 B–R3 R–B2 18 R–B1! (Simple chess. The idea is to win a pawn with B–B8) 18 ...N–K1 (or 18 ...R×R 19 K×R P–QN4 20 P–QN4! and 21 B–B8) 19 P–N3 B–N7 20 R×R N×R 21 B–B8 P–QN4 22 B–N6 winning at least one pawn.

(iii) 16 ...N–Q2 17 B–R3 R–B2 18 B×N! R×B 19 P–N3 P–QR3 20 R–B1. Winning the file and probably the game as well.

Although this does not exhaust Black's defensive possibilities, it does show that he has problems to solve. These problems arise primarily out of his inability to contest White's KR3–QB8 diagonal and the consequent difficulty in holding on to the QB file.

The minor pieces play a major role in determining who controls open files. The side with the more active minor pieces can gen-erally count on gaining access to any files that may open up. This is basically what happened in our previous examples. Naturally, outposts too have their part to play. This is better illustrated by diagram 37 than by words alone.

The main features of the position are an open QB file and a white outpost on QN6. The latter enables White to win the file in a

37

very straightforward manner: 1 N–R4 QR–B1 2 N–N6 R×R 3 R×R R–QN1 (what else?) 4 R–B7 N–K1 (what else?) 5 R–Q7 and Black has been totally run out of moves. The winning process for White is to centralise his king and then win the QP with N–B4. In the meantime Black has only waiting moves at his disposal.

Chess is very much a team game. The pieces rely heavily on each other's help and co-operation, so if one does not pull its weight it lets the whole side down. If you look back you will see that in no example so far has one side lost out on a file because his rooks were badly placed. In each case the team has been dragged down by the inability of some bishop or knight to match its opposite number. There is an old chess maxim: 'If one piece is bad, the whole position is bad.' How true. Maybe this will explain why there is so much talk of bishops, knights and kings (alas no cabbages!) in a chapter on open files.

38

There are, however, times when the major pieces have the right to determine their own destinies, and in these cases the first come, first served principle does operate. Diagram 38 shows a position structurally similar to a previous example of ours, but the presence of queens adds a new dimension.

1   N–Q5

As before White uses this move to force open the QB file, but this time simply because his heavy pieces are much better placed to contest the file than his opponent's. In particular, the black queen is horribly out of play on KR4.

1   ...   N×N

Again there is little choice in the matter. The white knight is too strong to be allowed to stay on the board.

2 BP×N QR–B1
3 R–B3!

Ensuring control of the file. The bleak position of the black queen means that White can dominate through sheer weight of numbers.

3 ... B×B
4 R×B Q–R3

Scuttling back into play, but the file is already lost.

5 R(Q2)–QB2 Q–B1
6 P–QR4

Superfluous. The immediate R–B7 is called for.

6 ... Q–K1
7 R–B7! R×R
8 R×R R–N1

The power of a rook on the seventh rank. It ties down both the black major pieces single-handed.

9 Q–B3

A multi-purpose move. White consolidates his grip on the file, at the same time threatening Q–N4 which stretches Black's defences to the limit.

9 Q–Q1
10 P–K5

Opening new avenues of attack. White can afford the luxury of this aggressive, but weakening move only because the opposing forces are totally immobilised.

10 ... P–QR3

Preparing to open some lines for his own pieces with ...P–QN4. If Black could ever break out of his strait-jacket, White's king would be a sitting duck.

11 P–KR4!

With P–R5–R6 in mind. Black lacks the manpower to defend both his pawns and his king.

11 ... P–QN4
12 R–B6

Seizing upon the negative aspect of Black's quest for freedom, White gains the use of the QB6 square as an outpost.

54 Open files

12	...	P×RP
13	P×RP	P×P
14	Q×P	R–B1

The QRP is taboo. 15 R×P? R–B7+ 16 K–R3 Q–B1+. As already remarked, White must keep a firm grip on the position because his king is potentially vulnerable.

15 P–KN4!

Turning the vague possibility of P–R5–R6 into reality.

Notice White's use of QB6 as an outpost. Black dare not trade rooks because the resulting passed pawn would soon queen. As a result the white rook can enjoy permanent residence there without fear of removal or exchange.

15	...	P–K3

39

A desperate try to undermine the rook. He otherwise lacks a good defence to P–R5–R6.

16 Q–B3! R×R

Equivalent to resignation, but there is no alternative. 16 ...R–N1 17 P×P P×P 18 R–B7 leads to mate or win of queen.

17 P×R K–B1?

And now a simple blunder, but after the forced 17 ...Q–B2 18 P–QR5 (threatening Q–B5–N6) K–B1 19 Q–N4+ K–K1 20 Q–N7! K–Q1 (20 ...Q×RP 21 P–B7 Q–Q7+ 22 K–R3) 21 Q×P and White must win.

18	P–B7	Q–B1
19	Q–R8+ and Black resigned.	

One of the dangers of falling behind in development in the opening is that the enemy rooks will be first on the scene and will take possession of the open files before your own can be scrambled into action. Rooks are notoriously difficult to bring into play quickly, so any loss of time incurred early on is liable to postpone their development still further. Many games have been won or lost because of this, but few display this motif with subtlety of the following encounter.

40 White: U. Andersson, Black: R. Knaak. Capablanca Memorial Tournament, 1974
1 N–KB3 N–KB3 2 P–B4 P–QN3 3 P–KN3 B–N2 4 B–N2 P–B4 5 0–0 P–N3 6 P–N3 B–N2 7 B–N2 0–0 8 N–B3 N–K5 9 Q–B2 N×N 10 B×N B×B 11 Q×B P–Q4?!

The exchanges initiated by Black's eighth move have left him slightly behind in development. As a result he should try to keep the position closed with 11 ...P–Q3. White now takes the opportunity to open up the game, which in turn enables him to be first to the central files with his rooks.

12 P–Q4! P×QP
13 Q×P P×P
14 Q×BP N–B3
15 KR–Q1

In simple near-symmetrical positions the advantage of the move can be considerable. Here Black has problems finding a hideout for his queen, e.g. 15 ...Q–B2? 16 N–Q4 QR–B1 17 B×N B×B 18 QR–B1 KR–Q1 19 N×B R×R+ 20 R×R Q×B 21 R–Q8+!

15 ... Q–K1
16 Q–B4!

The strongest and aesthetically most pleasing moves in chess are often very quiet ones. This innocent-looking queen move suddenly renders Black's position most precarious. With possibilities of an invasion on QB7 or KR6, Black must tread warily.

16 ...   R–B1

Eliminating one of the threats, while 17 Q–R6 can be met by P–B3. 16 ...P–K4 was unfortunately impossible because of 17 N×P!

17 R–Q2!

Another mouse-like move with the strength of a lion. White doubles on the Q file because he can see an entry point on Q7.

17 ...   K–N2

Clearly worried about the constant 'threat' of Q–R6. The alternative, 17 ...P–B3 (threatening P–K4–K5), is hardly inviting after 18 B–R3! R–Q1 19 B–K6+ K–N2 20 QR–Q1 R×R 21 R×R N–Q1 22 N–Q4.

18 QR–Q1 B–R1

Finally threatening P–K4–K5, but White has a very simple reply.

19 N–K5   N×N
20 Q×N+ P–B3

Or 20 ...K–N1 also sees White's major pieces penetrating in classic style: 21 B×B R×B 22 R–Q7 P–K3 23 Q–B6! followed by R–K7 and R(1)–Q7.

21 Q–K6   B×B
22 R–Q7!

41

The triumphant entrance! We now see the immense power of a rook on the seventh row.

22 ...   R–KB2
23 K×B   R–B4

He cannot avoid losing a pawn. His position after 23 ...R–R1 24 R–B7 and R(1)–Q7 would be laughable.

24 R×P   P–QN4

An amusing alternative is 24 ...R–K4 25 Q×QNP R×P 26 R–Q8! checkmating the queen.

25 P–K3

At this point Black acknowledged the hopelessness of his cause by resigning, hardly a premature decision as he has a pawn less and no constructive moves at all. A possible continuation would be 25 ...R–K4 26 Q–N6 (threatening R–Q8) R–B1 27 R(1)–Q7 and Q–B7.

To summarise, the use of open files can be broken down into three parts:

(i) Take control of the file.

(ii) Find a point of entry (this is the important part; without an entry point a file has no value).

(iii) Penetrate via the entry point.

Obviously no steadfast rules can be laid down about what to do after stage (iii). You just have to play it by ear. In the majority of cases, however, the right plan is readily apparent. To round off our discussion of open files, we look at an endgame from Karpov–Uhlmann, Madrid 1973, which exhibits a very common product of open file play, doubled rooks on the seventh rank.

42

Here White (to move) controls the king file, because of his powerful bishop outpost on N5. Indeed his entire advantage can be ascribed to the superiority of his minor piece over its opposite number. The black bishop has no outpost as it can be driven away from K5.

1 P–B3   B–N3
2 R–K7

The entry point.

2 ...   P–N3
3 QR–K1

More accurate than 3 R–N7 R–B7. He gives Black no chance to counter-penetrate by exploiting the back row weakness (3 ...R–B1 4 R–K8+).

3 ...   P–KR3
4 R–N7   R–Q3

Passive defence. More competitive but insufficient is 4 ...R–B7 viz. 5 R(1)–K7 (The QNP is not important. What is important is to prise open the seventh rank for his rooks.) 5 ...R×P 6 B–K8 R–B1! (also playing for doubled rooks on the seventh) 7 B×P+ B×B 8 R×B R(1)–B7 9 R×P+ K–B1 10 K–R2! (were he to allow his king to be trapped on the back rank, White would be unable to win) 10 ...R×P+ 11 K–R3 White's king can now escape the checks and his own rook triumphs, e.g. 11 ...R–R7+ 12 K–N3 R(R7)–N7+ 13 K–B4 R–N5 14 R–KR7! K–N1 (14 ...R×QP+ 15 K–K5!) 15 R(R7)–Q7 and wins.

5 R(1)–K7   P–KR4

This time 5 ...R–B7 loses a pawn to 6 R–N8+ K–R2 7 R(K7)–K8 R–B8+ 8 K–R2 B–N8 (forced to avoid mate) 9 R–R8+ K–N3 10 R(R8)–Q8! e.g. 10 ...R×R 11 R×R B–R7 12 R–Q6+.

6 P×P   B×P
7 P–KN4 B–N3
8 P–B4!

In order to open the seventh rank for his rooks, White must drive the bishop from its defence of KB2. The direct 8 B–K8 can be met by R–KB3.

8 ...   R–B8+
9 K–B2   R–B7+
10 K–K3   B–K5

He can no longer hold the KB2 point—10 ...R–B3 11 P–B5 B–R2 12 R–K8 mate.

11 R×KBP R–N3
12 P–N5 K–R2

The immediate 12 ...R×QNP leads to much the same result after 13 R(B7)–K7 threatening B–K8.

13 R(B7)–K7 R×QNP
14 B–K8

Clearing the final obstacle to White's total domination of the seventh rank.

14 ... R–N6+
15 K–K2 R–N7+
16 K–K1 R–Q3

The checks won't last for ever, e.g. 16 ...R–N8+ 17 K–Q2 R–N7+ 18 K–B3 R–B7+ 19 K–N3.

17 R×P+ K–R1
18 R(KN7)–K7 Black resigns.

When the checks run out White's mating threats (R–N8 and B moves) are unstoppable.

5. Half-open files: the minority attack

The open file is a double-edged weapon. Although a way to feed the major pieces into the heart of the opponent's position, there is always the danger of it being seized and used to reciprocal effect by the enemy. In short, it is a two-way road for rooks. The chessplayer, not being an unselfish advocate of equality of opportunity, naturally prefers a one-way system. The half-open file is precisely this. We do not have to go very far (three moves to be exact) to find an example of one: 1 P–Q4 P–Q4 2 P–QB3 P–K3 3 P×P P×P. ·

43

White has the half-open QB file, Black the half-open K file. So what does this mean? Cannot Black always erect a granite wall on the QB file by P–QB3 and White do similarly on the K file by P–K3 ? Yes of course, but the point is that the black pawn chain QN2, QB3, Q4 can be challenged by White with P–QN4–N5. When P–N5 comes, there is no way Black can avoid being left with a weak pawn. If he captures away from QB3, the queen's pawn is left isolated, while allowing an exchange on his QB3 will leave the QBP backward. These are the simple mechanics of the *minority attack*. It is no more nor less than a method of weakening an otherwise sound pawn set-up by advancing pawns at it. The process is quite long and slow, the payoff at the end relatively small (one weak pawn to aim at, two maybe if you are lucky), but its value is undeniable. Moreover, it cannot easily rebound on you. An open file can change hands, a half-open file cannot. Indeed it cannot even be challenged. Imagine the contortions Black would have to go through to oppose rooks on the QB file in front of his pawns in a position akin to that of diagram 43. Out of the question. The minority attack has a certain inevitability about it. Though cumbersome, once the mighty wheels have been set in motion, the opposition has no way to apply the brakes.

So much for extolling the virtues of half-open files, but going back to diagram 43 we see that Black has the K file. Surely he too can launch a minority attack in due course? Not so easy. A minority attack on the king's file would involve advancing his KB and KN pawns. But where is he to put his king? Certainly not on the queenside in the path of White's attack. On the other hand it is not the height of expediency to castle kingside and then send your kingside pawns scampering off into the distance to create just one weak pawn in the enemy camp. The final reward is simply not worth the risk. In general one cannot afford to mount a minority attack in front of a castled king. These attacks only usually work on the other side of the board.

Let us look at a couple of examples of play from diagram 43 to see how the minority attacks work out in practice.

44 1 P–Q4 P–Q4 2 P–QB4 P–K3 3 P×P P×P 4 N–QB3 N–KB3 5 B–N5 B–K2 6 P–K3 P–B3 7 Q–B2 0–0 8 B–Q3 QN–Q2 9 N–B3 R–K1 10 0–0 N–B1 11 QR–N1.

This is a standard position in the so-called (for obvious reasons) Exchange Variation of the Queen's Gambit. White's method of development is both simple and economical, and with his last move he prepares to set the minority attack in motion, by P–QN4. Black's method of play has been a little more contorted (R–K1, N–B1), the reason being that not having a worthwhile minority attack of his own, he wants to channel as many pieces as possible over to the kingside in order to create some diversionary threats there.

Our first example, Van den Berg-Kramer 1950, proceeded

11 ... P–KN3

So as to play N–K3 without losing a pawn to B×N.

12 P–QN4 P–QR3
13 P–QR4 N–K3
14 B–R4

No need to rush things with 14 B×N B×B 15 P–N5. In fact after 15 ...RP×P 16 RP×P P–B4! 17 P×P N×P Black is becoming quite active (he threatens N×B and B–B4).

14 ... N–N2
15 P–N5 RP×P
16 RP×P B–B4

Black's lengthy manoeuvres have been designed to exchange this piece, always a problem child in the Queen's Gambit.

17 P×P P×P
18 N–K5

Beginning to harvest the fruits of his queenside campaign.

18 ... R–QB1
19 R–N7

A useful fringe benefit. White has first crack at the newly opened QN file. Notice the way his pieces have gained momentum in the wake of the advancing pawns.

19 ... B×B
20 Q×B R–B2

White was threatening 21 B×N B×B 22 N×KBP.

21 R×R Q×R
22 R–B1

With the new threat 23 B×N B×B 24 N×QP.

22 ... Q–N2
23 Q–N1! Q–R3

23 ...Q×Q 24 N×Q wins a pawn.

24 N–R2

And White is winning the QBP, e.g. 24 ...R–QB1 25 B×N B×B 26 N–N4 etc.

If Black is unable to throw any tactical spanners in the works, the well-oiled, mechanical minority attack will generally swallow up a pawn sooner or later.

Our second example shows how to create counterplay against the minority attack. Resuming from the position of diagram 44

11	...	P–QR4
12	P–QR3	N–K5
13	B×B	Q×B
14	P–QN4	P×P
15	P×P	N–N3
16	P–N5	B–N5

45

Black is feeding pieces over to the kingside much more efficiently than in the previous example. White must now proceed with caution. On 17 N–Q2?, there comes 17 ...N×N(Q7) 18 Q×N N–R5. The powerful threats 19 ...B–R6! and 19 ...B–B6! leave White at a loss for a reasonable reply, e.g. 19 P–B3 Q×P+! 20 Q×Q R×Q 21 P×B R×B.

Even here, however, White can extract something from the position by judicious play, i.e. 17 B×N! P×B 18 N–Q2 B–B4 19 P×P P×P 20 N–K2 with threats of Q×BP or N–N3. The two knights do a good job here, hopping in and out of the weak squares created by White's queenside advance. The minority attack is not purely geared to producing weak pawns, but creates outposts as well (QB5 in this case).

Given that a minority attack runs more smoothly away from the central files (we saw in our previous examples that White could operate a minority attack with some effect on the QB file, whereas Black found it difficult to get going on the K file), and the startling criterion that a pawn minority is needed for a minority attack, it is not difficult to appreciate that the best place to acquire a pawn majority is in the centre. A surplus of pawns in the middle necessarily means a deficit somewhere else (assuming of course both sides do have equal pawns). Remember the old rule 'always capture towards the centre' applying to a choice of pawn captures. The advantage of the central pawn majority is the *raison d'être* for this piece of advice. The hidden implication is: accumulate pawns in the centre and you can start minority attacks on the flanks.

Take the following variation of the English Opening: 1 P–QB4 N–KB3 2 N–QB3 P–Q4 3 P×P N×P 4 P–KN3 P–KN3 5 B–N2 N×N 6 NP×N B–N2.

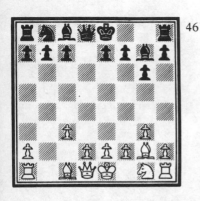

46

By recapturing the knight 'towards the centre' (i.e. with the NP rather than the QP), White has given himself an extra central pawn. The offshoot of this is a half-open QN file which can later on in the game be used for a minority attack. To this end he does well to adopt a solid but purely passive pawn set-up in the centre (say pawns on K2, Q3, QB4) so as to be able to direct all his fire-power to the left flank later on. Diagram 47 shows the type of position that might occur later on after some exchanges. White is ready to launch his minority attack.

1   P–QR4   P–K3

Black wants to hold his queenside together by N–Q2 without allowing a white knight to jump into Q5.

2   P–R5   N–Q2

Taking the QRP would split up Black's pawns too much, e.g. 2 ...P×P? 3 N–N5 Q–K2 4 R×P and the other QRP will not last long either.

3   P×P   P×P

4   R(3)–R3

With an obvious invasion threat on the seventh rank. Despite only having one file and one weakness to work on, White can make life very uncomfortable for his opposite number.

4   ...   Q–B3

The passive 4 ...R–N1 5 R–R7 R–N2 is hopeless viz. 6 N–N5 Q–N1 7 R×R Q×R 8 R–R7 Q–B1 9 N–Q6 Q–Q1 10 R–N7 followed by Q–N5 will win the QNP with the prospect of more to come.

5   R–R7   R–R1

6   N–K4

The tremor of White's queenside activity is gradually beginning to be felt right across the board. The immediate threat is 7 R×N! followed by N–B6+. It is very interesting the way a single weakness can spread disease throughout the entire position (as a result of one backward pawn on QN3, Black now finds his king under direct threat).

6   ...   R×R

Against the immediate 6 ...P–B4, White can win a pawn as follows: 7 R×R R×R 8 R×R+ Q×R 9 Q–N5! P×N (9 ...Q–Q1? 10 Q×N) 10 Q×N Q–R8+ 11 K–N2 Q–K4 12 Q–Q8+ K–N2 13 Q×NP.

7 R×R   P–B4

The knight must be dislodged. 7 ...R–R1 8 R×R+ Q×R 9 Q–N5 sees Black going down without a fight (9 ...Q–Q1? 10 Q×N).

8 N–N5   P–KR3
9 Q–N5!   Q×Q
10 P×Q   P×N
11 R×N

The dust clears leaving White with a superactive rook which should lead to the win of at least a pawn in the ensuing endgame, e.g. 11 ...R–R1 12 R–Q6 or 11 ...R–N1 12 R–K7.

So what part, if any, does the central pawn majority play in the minority attack? A considerable part. The plan of seeping into the Black position via the queenside is essentially slow and non-forcing. It only succeeds because Black has no point to counter-attack, and this in turn is due to the impervious white centre. Minority attacks must be built on the foundations of a firm central position. The victory may be won on the flank, but ultimately it is created in the centre.

Minority attacks derive from the pawn structure, pawn structures derive from the opening. Go back to the eras of Capablanca and Alekhine and you will see Queen's Gambits, hoards of them, with hoards of minority attacks descending from them. Nowadays the Sicilian Defence is all the rage. Sicilians here, Sicilians there, Sicilians absolutely everywhere. Why this saturation with Sicilians? Does the Mafia's influence really extend this far? The answer lies in the minority attack. The whole idea of the Sicilian is for Black to trade his QBP for the QP. White almost invariably obliges 1 P–K4 P–QB4 2 N–KB3 N–QB3 (or P–Q3 or P–K3 or P–KN3) 3 P–Q4 P×P, when Black immediately arrives at a minority attack pawn structure. Half-open QB file, extra central pawn, 2–3 minority on the queenside; these are all the necessary ingredients. Sounds infallible, so where's the snag? Why doesn't Black win every game? The problem is of course that White has a lead in development in the early stages, which may prove difficult to survive. Black's prospects lie later in the game when the winds of White's initiative have blown themselves out.

48 White: L. Vogt, Black: U. Andersson.
Havana 1975
1 P–K4 P–QB4 2 N–KB3 P–Q3 3 P–Q4 P×P 4 N×P N–KB3 5 N–QB3 P–K3 6 B–K2 P–QR3 7 P–B4 Q–B2 8 0–0 B–K2 9 K–R1 N–B3 10 B–K3 N×N 11 Q×N 0–0 12 QR–Q1 P–QN4

A fairly typical Sicilian position. White has more space and better development, but Black is solidly placed. His last move does give a hint of the minority attack one day to come, but his primary concern for the moment is to complete his development before a tactical accident befalls him.

13 P–K5

Trying to precipitate an accident.

13 ... P×P
14 Q×P

A devious attempt to exploit Black's lag in development. The idea lies in 14 ...Q×Q 15 P×Q N–Q2 16 B–B3 R–N1 17 B–R7 slaying the rook in its bed. However, Black has an equally devious response up his sleeve.

14 ... Q–N1!

She who turns and runs away saves her rook for later play. Now 15 B–B3 can be simply met by B–N2.

15 Q×Q

White suddenly finds his box of tricks empty and so submits to an exchange of queens, but the endgame gives Black an excellent opportunity to play his minority attack.

15 ... R×Q
16 B–R7 R–R1
17 B–N6 B–N2
18 P–QR3 KR–B1!

A good time to compare the relative values of open and half-open files. White has the Q file (his BN6 sees to that), but no entry point, no threats, no pressure. Black has the half-open QB file. He threatens . . . B×RP, undermining the knight. The knight cannot move away because it is 'pinned' in front of the QBP. Half-open files do not need entry points. They naturally generate pressure.

19 B–QR5

Bolstering the threatened knight.

19 . . .   P–N3

A useful little move. White's pawn on KB4 is something of a liability and Black intends to keep it there as such.

20 P–KR3?

The psychological effect of a waiting move pays immediate dividends. As in trench warfare the worst part of defending against a minority attack is waiting for it to come. White wants to free his back rank from possible threats later on, but in doing so weakens his kingside pawns too much. Better is 20 B–N4.

20 . . .   P–KR4!

Heading for R5 to isolate the white KBP from its KNP. This advance ensures that Black will have targets on both sides of the board to aim at.

21 B–B3   B×B
22 R×B   P–R5!
23 R–Q2   R–B5

49

Showing yet another feature of the half-open file, the outpost on B5. Not an outpost in the strict sense of the word as White can drive the rook away, but only at the cost of severely weakening his defences on the QB file.

24   P–QN3

Undesirable, but forced. There is no other way to counter the plan of ...QR–B1 (pinning the knight in front of the QBP) and ...N–R4 winning the KBP. Notice the way Black uses a pawn weakness on the kingside (KB4) to engineer a weakening of the queenside (P–QN3).

24   ...   R–B3
25   P–QR4   P–N5
26   N–K2   QR–B1

The minority attack has done its job. White is left with a backward QBP.

27   P–B4

This solves his problems on the QB file only to create a fresh weakness on the QN file. The logical way to defend is to try and trade rooks by 27 N–Q4 R–B6 28 R×R R×R 29 R–Q3 R×R 30 P×R, but even this fails to save White as his pawns are too split, viz. 30 ...N–Q4 31 N–K2 B–Q3 32 K–B1 B×P! 33 N×B N×N 34 B×P N×QP 35 B–K7 P–B4 36 B×P N–B4! and Black emerges with an extra pawn.

27   ...   P×P e.p.
28   R×P   N–Q4
29   R×R   R×R

50

The beginning of a new phase. White has two weaknesses (KB4, QN3) one as a result of the minority attack, one as a result of his own ineptitude (20 P–KR3?). Black's task is now to attack each in turn and thereby completely tie down the white forces. There is no counterplay to reckon with, the dominating knight sees to that.

30 R–N2

A doomed attempt to straighten his queenside out with P–QN4.

30 ... B–B3

31 R–R2 R–B1

To transfer to the QN file. Still more convincing is the little combination 31 ...N×P! 32 N×N R–B8+ 33 K–R2 B–K4 35 B–Q2 R–Q8 when the twin threats of ...R×B and ...P–N4 enable Black to recover his investment with a reasonable rate of interest.

32 B–Q2 R–N1

33 N–B1 N–N5

34 B×N R×B

The outpost in front of the backward pawn.

35 R–KB2 B–K2

36 R–B3 B–Q3

37 N–K2

Everything miraculously still defended, but White is reduced to total passivity.

37 ... R–K5

38 R–Q3

Again the only way to avoid immediate material loss (38 R–B2 B–B4).

38 ... B–B4

39 R–QB3 B–B7

40 R–B2 K–N2

The time is ripe for the king to march in. All the white pieces are amusingly trapped, like a bicycle wheel in a tramline, only able to go backwards and forwards.

41 N–N1

Rather than submit to the humiliation of idling his king to and fro while the black monarch strides in and mops up, White surrenders a pawn to free his pieces, but to no avail of course.

41 ... R×P and Black soon won.

The pawn structure, or rather distribution in this endgame, is well worth remembering. Black had a 4–3 majority on the kingside (KP, KBP, KNP, KRP *v.* KBP, KNP, KRP) and White a 3–2 surplus on the queenside (QBP, QNP, QRP *v.* QNP, QRP). This distribution is fundamentally favourable for Black, firstly because of his extra central pawn (which in the game provided him with a powerful outpost on Q4 for his knight), and secondly because of the queenside minority attack. There is also a third advantage not apparent from our last game: four pawns protect a king better than three. How many times have you read that Black's classical freeing move in the Sicilian is . . .P–Q4 without understanding why? If Black can swap his QP for White's KP he reaches the 4–3 *v*. 2–3 distribution advertised above. Of course if White can meet . . .P–Q4 with P–K5 it's a different story. . . .

The Sicilian is not the only opening geared to reach this pawn distribution. For example the following line of the Caro-Kann 1 P–K4 P–QB3 2 P–Q4 P–Q4 3 N–QB3 P×P 4 N×P N–Q2 5 B–QB4 KN–B3 6 N–N5 P–K3 7 Q–K2 N–N3 8 B–Q3 P–KR3 9 N(5)–B3 P–QB4 sees Black liquidating the white QP to achieve the desired pawn set-up. Similarly in the French Defence 1 P–K4 P–K3 2 P–Q4 P–Q4 3 N–QB3 P×P 4 N×P N–Q2 5 N–KB3 KN–B3 Black soon gets in P–QB4. These openings have failed to supersede the Sicilian in popularity only because they are more difficult to handle. Although Black obtains the pawn formation he wants much faster, he can experience great difficulties in developing his queenside. This is always the price paid for freeing your game too quickly in these openings. If Black can, however, succeed in bringing all his pieces into play unscarred he is assured of an equal game —at least. The struggle to develop can lead to very sharp play.

51 White: M. Stean, Black: A. J. Mestel
1 P–K4 P–K3 2 P–Q4 P–Q4 3 N–Q2 P–QB4 4 KP×P Q×P 5 KN–B3 P×P 6 B–B4 Q–Q3 7 0–0 N–QB3 8 N–N3 N–B3 9 QN×P N×N 10 N×N B–Q2 11 B–N3 Q–B2

A now familiar pawn set-up, but Black's many queen moves have left him dangerously behind in development. His last move however prepares . . .B–Q3 bringing a piece into play with tempo. If he can safely castle, Black will stand well.

12 B–N5

Crossing Black's plans. 12 ...B–Q3 is met by 13 B×N P×B (13 ...B×P+ 14 K–R1 P×B 15 P–N3 wins a piece) 14 Q–R5 and the black king has no safe haven.

12 ... N–K5

A bold reply. The quiet 12 ...B–K2 fails to solve all the problems in view of 13 R–K1 0–0 14 N–B5!

13 B–R4 B–Q3

14 Q–N4!?

Striving hard to keep the initiative. The more conservative 14 N–B3 0–0 15 R–K1 N–B4 allows Black the type of position he is aiming for.

14 ... B×P+

15 K–R1 Q–B5!

16 Q×NP

The only consistent continuation, but it runs the gauntlet of Black's dangerous attack.

16 ... Q×B

17 Q×R+ K–K2

Threatens both mate and the queen. Maybe White has overplayed his hand?

18 N–B3!

Temporary salvation at least.

18 ... Q–R3

The startling 18 ...Q×P works after 19 R×Q N×R+ 20 K×B R×Q, but after the simple 19 Q×R Black has amazingly enough no mate.

19 Q×R

52

Into the valley of death, or so it seems. But where is the mate? 19
...B–Q3+ 20 K–N1 N–Q7 21 KR–Q1! N×N+ 22 P×N Q–R7+
23 K–B1 B–N4+ 24 P–B4 and Black has only one more check for
his huge material deficit. Could it be that the whole attack is
nothing more than an optical illusion and that White has been
winning all along?

19   ...   N–N6+!

Not quite.

20 P×N   B×P+
21 K–N1   Q–K6+
22 K–R1   Q–R3+   Draw!

An entertaining miniature typical of the modern trend. Complications not for complication's sake, but to pre-empt the minority attack which would certainly have later come, had Black been
given time to consolidate by castling.

The one aspect of the half-open file not properly covered to
date is the outpost on the half-open file. This is best explained by
an example.

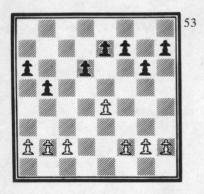

53

Diagram 53 shows another typical Sicilian pawn structure. Black
has the half-open QB file, White the Q file. Each has an associated
outpost, White on Q5, Black on QB5. Outpost is something of a
misnomer here, for as you may remember an outpost was orig-
inally defined as a square that could not be challenged by an
enemy pawn. Here Black can play P–K3 and White P–QN3
challenging the respective outposts, but only at a cost. P–QN3
weakens the QB3 square and so makes the QBP pawn more
difficult to defend. Correspondingly, P–K3 weakens the black

QP, so these moves can only be made in exceptional circumstances. The squares Q5 (White's) and QB5 (Black's) are therefore effectively outposts, if not technically so.

These considerations explain a couple of points about the Sicilian Defence that may have been puzzling you:

(i) Why does Black so often develop his KB passively with P–K3 and B–K2 when he can give it a beautiful diagonal by P–KN3 and B–N2 ? Because P–K3 and B–K2 deprive White of his Q5 outpost without leaving the QP too weak. After P–KN3 and B–N2 Black can rarely consider P–K3 as well.

(ii) Why is the Maroczy Bind (pawns on K4 and QB4) considered so effective for White against the Sicilian? Because with a white pawn on QB4 Black can have no outpost there, and Black can generate very little play on the QB file.

Strategical problems are born in the opening, which is why it is so important to *understand* the openings you play. Hopefully this chapter has given you some insight into the workings of the Sicilian Defence and related openings as well as the minority attack.

6. Black squares and white squares

Pawns are quite happy to defend pieces (outposts), yet pieces do not enjoy being tied to the defence of pawns (weak pawns). Bear these simple principles in mind and you are well on the way to mastering one of the fundamental problems of chess—co-operation between pieces and pawns. This harmony between workers and management so to speak is not solely the responsibility of the shop floor. There is no such thing as the 'perfect' pawn formation, because different pieces react in different ways to the same pawn skeleton. One of the arts of chess strategy is to recognise which of your pieces fit in well with the pawn structure, and to exchange off the ones that do not. In this context we are referring primarily to minor pieces (i.e. bishops and knights).

Recognition of pieces which do or do not fit in well with the pawn structure centres mainly around the concept of 'good' and 'bad' bishops. If most of your central pawns become blocked on black squares, say, the future for your black-squared bishop on the other hand will be completely unimpaired by its pawns. Moreover, pawns on black squares do not protect white squares, so the bishop is also needed to help cover the 'gaps'. Knights are less likely to be brought up before the Race Relations Board for colour consciousness. They are quite happy to hop from black squares to white and back again.

54

Diagram 54 is a typical case of good bishop v. bad bishop. The pawn structure is entirely symmetrical, but White's bishop is compatible with his pawn structure whereas Black's is a prisoner in his own camp. White wins without effort:

1 Q–Q5+ Q×Q
2 KP×Q

He recaptures this way to vacate K4 for his king.

2 ... B–Q3

Black would like to release his bishop with 2 ...P–K5, but the threat of B–Q2 (yet another pawn on a black square) precludes this.

3 K–B3 K–B2
4 K–K4 K–B3
5 B–Q2 B–B2
6 B–B3

Not the only way to win. Equally efficient is 6 P–Q6 B×P (6 ...B–Q1 7 K–Q5 etc.) 7 B×P any 8 B–B3 any 9 P–R5 any 10 P–R6 B–QN1 11 B×P+! making a new queen.

6 ... P–R3

Black has only waiting moves.

7 P–R3 P–R4
8 P–R4

Zugzwang. Any move by Black loses at least a pawn.

Many people reason 'If I put my pawns on the same coloured squares as my bishop I can defend them there'. If you commit *hara-kiri* instead, you won't have to defend them at all. The two solutions are roughly equivalent, give or take the problem of cleaning the blood off the board. The real fallacy in the argument is that if you put all your pawns on squares of the same colour, say black, there is no defence against enemy penetration on the white squares. Look at diagram 55.

There is only very scanty material left on the board and Black has only one pawn to keep protected. Yet his position is hopeless because he cannot prevent the white king penetrating on the light squares B5, K6, Q7:

1 B–B2!

A quiet move typical of these endgames. White could win a piece by 1 B–N6 K–B3 2 B–N8 K–K3 3 P–N6 P×P 4 P–B7, but this only leads to a draw—4 ...B×P 5 B×B P–Q4.

55

1 ...　K–N2

Black is forced to give way. Any bishop move is answered by 2 P–N6 P×P 3 P–B7, while 1 ...K–B3? loses the bishop (2 B–R4+).

2　K–B5　K–B2

The second line of defence.

3　B–K3

Once again forcing a king move in reply, bishop moves being met by P–N6.

3　...　K–K2

Or 3 ...K–K1 4 K–K6 and Black is in zugzwang again.

4　B–N5+ K–K1
5　K–K6!!

5 B×B also wins, but the text move is both more thematic and more aesthetic.

5　...　B×B
6　P–N6

And White gets a new queen for Christmas: 6 ...P×P 7 P–B7 or 6 ...B–Q1 (or K–Q1) 7 P–N7.

This is what we are talking about when we say things like '.... and Black is weak on the white squares'. We mean there is a danger that a king (in the endgame) or a queen (in the late middlegame) will be able to penetrate into the position. Using bridge parlance, he has a duplication of honours. His pawns cover black squares, his bishop does the same, so that after suitable exchanges there will be little more than an overworked king to guard the other thirty-two.

Naturally the less material on the board, the clearer the bad bishop syndrome. This is why we started the section with two examples of pure bishop endgames. With rooks on as well however the overall strategy is much the same.

56

Diagram 56 shows an endgame (Tarrasch-Teichmann) which all exponents of the French Defence should try to avoid. Black has a bad bishop and weak black squares. The execution runs as follows:

1   P–KN4

The key to the white position is his king's outpost on Q4. Because Black has no minor piece able to operate on black squares, he cannot usurp the white monarch from its throne and moreover must keep a rook permanently stationed on the QB file to prevent his majesty from walking in. You may remember that the 'weakness' of weak pawns was that pieces could be tied down to their defence. Similarly the 'weakness' of weak squares is that defending pieces must keep them permanently covered to prevent infiltration. To exploit this constraint on the mobility of the black rooks, White must bring his own into the game. This he does by a general advance on the kingside which will eventually lead to the opening of some lines there. He chooses the extreme right flank for this action to stretch the defence as much as possible. In endgames you should try to introduce 'width' into your play, i.e. create trouble on two widely-spaced fronts.

1   ...   B–B1

2 P–KR4 P–N3

Trying to keep the kingside closed. Against purely waiting tactics White would continue R–KN1 and P–N5, meeting ...P–KR4 with P–N6.

3 R–R1 K–N2

4 P–R5 R–R1

He cannot barricade the kingside by 4 ...P–N4 because of 5 P×P P×P 6 P–R6+ K–N1 7 R–R5 etc.

5 R(B2)–R2 B–Q2

6 P–N5

Opening the king's wing by force, thus enabling his rooks to get their teeth into Black's position.

6 ... RP×P

7 BP×P P×P

8 R×P R×R

9 R×R

57

A good point for a brief resumé on the state of play. White has secured an open file *plus* an entry point (R7), while the black rook is still playing the role of nightwatchman. Initially White had the better bishop, now he has the better rook as well.

9 ... K–B1

10 R–R8+ K–K2

11 P–N6

Opening up the seventh rank for his rook.

11 ... P×P

12 B×P P–N5

80 Black squares and white squares

In principle the right idea—establish pawns on *black* squares wherever possible—but here it hardly helps at all.

13   R–R7+

A mistake. He should not encourage the black king to run over to the queenside where it can relieve the rook from its job of custodian of the black squares (QB4 in particular). Correct is the immediate 13 B–Q3 leaving the black king hemmed in on K2.

13   ...   K–Q1

14   B–Q3?

He still had time to rectify his previous error by 14 R–R8+ and 15 B–Q3.

14   ...   R–B6?

There are good drawing chances after 14 ...R–B3! (vacating B2 for the king) 15 R–R8+ K–B2 16 R–R8 K–N2.

15   P–R3!

The vital difference. Black's RP is drawn forward to R4 where it is indefensible.

15   ...   P–R4

16   R–R8+ K–K2

Or 16 ...K–B2 17 R–R8 K–N3 18 R–R6+ wins the pawn anyway.

17   R–R8

and Black resigned as he is losing a pawn without any improvement in his position.

The natural corollary to these endgames is that if you have a bishop of one colour, it is imperative to establish pawns, particularly central pawns, on squares of the other colour. It can make the difference between a win and a loss.

For example, diagram 58 shows a position from the game Burn-Marshall, Ostend 1907. White (to move) has a strong central passed pawn, or is it strong? The answer depends on whether or not he can advance it. On Q5 it merely obstructs the bishop, on Q6 it is a giant. After the natural 1 P–Q6 P–B5 2 P×P P×P 3 Q–K7 (threat 4 P–Q7!) R–K1 4 Q–B7 White has all the chances. Instead, Burn chose the incomprehensible ...

1   Q–B3? Q×Q

2   R×Q

... allowing his pawn to be blocked on a white square.

2 ...   N–K1!

> Now Black is clearly in the driving seat. He is effectively at least half a pawn up, as the White QP is blocked and useless. Moreover the black squares are weak in as much as White has little to counter the black king marching to K4.

3   K–B1   K–B1
4   B–K2   N–Q3

> The ideal square for the knight. In a sense the White QP 'protects' the knight from harassment on the Q file.

5   R–B2   K–K2
6   R–R2

> The only way to activate the rook is round the back through the tradesman's entrance, but it's very slow.

6   ...   P–B5
7   P×P   P×P
8   K–K1   R–B4

> Underlining the sad decline in the fortunes of the once proud QP, now a miserable weakness.

9   B–B3   P–B6
10   K–Q1   N–N4
11   R–R4   K–Q3
12   R–R6+   K–K4
13   K–B1

> A better chance is 13 R–B6 using his outpost, the one remaining value of the passed pawn. After 13 ...K–Q5! however, White is still in difficulties:

(i) 14 K–B2 N–R6+ 15 K–B1 R–N4!

(ii) 14 R×R K×R 15 K–B2 N–Q5+! 16 K×P N×B 17 P×N K×P and White loses the K+P endgame because of his broken pawns viz. 17 K–Q3 K–K4 18 K–K3 P–N4! zugzwang.

13 ... N–Q5
14 P–Q6

A black square at last—but too late.

14 ... P–B7
15 R–R3 R–N4 and Black wins by force viz., 16 R–B3 R–N8+ 17 K–Q2 K×P 19 B–K4 P–B8=Q+ 20 R×Q N–N6+.

The most powerful piece in any endgame is the king, and the white square/black square strategy is aimed to carve out a route into the enemy camp for it. You can see the reason for stationing pawns on squares of colour opposite to that of your bishop by the following little exercise. Set up a white bishop on K4 and pawn on Q4 opposed by a black king on Q3. The king wants to cross the fourth rank. To do so, it must traverse as far as the KN file in one direction (K–K3–B3–N4) or the QR file in the other direction (K–B2–N3, at which point White can transfer the bishop to Q3, – R4). Thus we see that a white-squared bishop in conjunction with a black-squared pawn provides a pretty wide barrier against an enemy king. Now transfer the pawn on Q4 to a white square, any white square (e.g. Q5, QB4, Q3), and the king walks straight through. So in assessing how bad a bad bishop is, or equivalently how weak a weak square complex is with a view to the endgame, the main criterion must be: how easily can the opponent's king break in? Let us look at an exceptional example (diagram 59).

59

Black has the worst bishop the world has ever seen and four sick pawns to defend, yet he cannot lose! Why not? Because the white king can never enter. White can only attack various pawns with his bishop, at most two at a time, but the threats are easily parried. Without a king there is no way to win. Now remove the white pawn from K5. Despite now being a pawn down, White wins easily because his king can play its part:

1	K–K5	K–K2
2	B–Q3	K–B2
3	K–Q6	

The black squares!

3	...	B–N2
4	K–B7	B–R1
5	K–N8 wins everything.	

As a final example to emphasise the power of the king in the ending, we turn to one of Tal's early games, against Lisitsin in the 1956 Soviet Championships.

60

In diagram 60 Tal (White, to move) has all sorts of problems to solve with his ragged kingside pawns, but his opponent has some black square holes in the centre. The only way to play such endgames is to exploit your own advantages as vigorously as possible, even if it means total capitulation elsewhere. Here Tal decides to abandon his kingside to avoid being drawn into passive defence and concentrate all his efforts on the weak black squares.

1   P–B5!

Naturally he chooses the most unco-operative method of surrendering the kingside.

| 1 | ... | P×P |

Winning a pawn, but compromising his pawn structure to do so. He should instead be willing to fathom the murky depths of 1 ...N–N6 2 P–B6! R–K3 3 R–B3 N–K5.

2	R(B1)–K1	R(B1)–K1
3	R×R	R×R
4	K–Q2	

The beginning of the royal tour. Naturally the full consequences of such an adventure are not calculable, but calculation is not needed. Have faith in your king.

4	...	N–N6
5	K–B3	P–B5
6	K–Q4	B–B4

To create an entry point on K7 for his rook. Black has a pawn more and his pieces are very active, but he is playing without his king.

| 7 | R–Q2 | R–K3 |

Or 7 ...B×B 8 P×B R–K7 9 R×R N×R+ 10 K–B5 mopping up in the centre.

| 8 | N–B5 | R–R3 |
| 9 | K–K5! | |

The RP is going too, but no matter. The important point is that Black has no *passed* pawn to deflect the invading monarch.

9	...	B×B
10	P×B	R×P
11	K–Q6	R–R3+
12	K–B7	N–B4
13	K–N7	

Threatening to promote his QRP no less!

| 13 | ... | N–Q5 |
| 14 | R–B2 | |

Denying Black the chance to make any passed pawns by ...P–B6.

14	...	P–QR4
15	R×P	N–K3
16	R–N4+	K–B1
17	K×P	

His majesty now has the audacity to walk into a discovered check.

This is in fact the beginning of the end. White has recovered all his material and still has much the more active king.

17 ...   N×N+
18 K×N   R–K3
19 K×P and the rest is technique:

19 ...R–QN3 20 P–N4 P×P 21 P×P K–K2 22 K–B5 R–KB3 23 R–Q4 R–B4+ 24 K–N6 R–B3+ 25 K–B7 R–B4 26 R–K4+ K–B3 27 K–B6 R–B7 28 P–N4 P–R4 29 P×P K–N4 30 P–N5 P–B4 31 R–N4 P–B5 32 P–N6 P–B6 33 P–N7 Black resigns.

Before the endgame God made the middlegame and an opening to lead into it. Here the seeds of these colour strategies are sown. As soon as the central pawn set-ups crystallise into some sort of permanent structure, the respective good and bad bishops become self-evident. For example, the French Defence usually creates the pawn centres Q4, K5 (White) v. Q4, K3 (Black) in which cases each side has a 'bad' QB. Hence the opening variations:

1 P–K4 P–K3 2 P–Q4 P–Q4 3 N–QB3 N–KB3 4 B–N5 B–K2 5 P–K5 KN–Q2 6 B×B trading his bad bishop for Black's good one: or 1 P–K4 P–K3 2 P–Q4 P–Q4 3 N–QB3 B–N5 4 P–K5 P–QN3 preparing B–R3. Here Black is willing to meet 5 Q–N4 by ...B–B1, losing two tempi to secure the exchange of his bad bishop without giving up the good one (i.e. the KB); another idea is 1 P–K4 P–K3 2 P–Q4 P–Q4 3 P–K5 P–QB4 4 P–QB3 Q–N3 5 N–B3 B–Q2 followed by ...B–N4. Black's idea is always a white square strategy, i.e. exchange his QB for the opposing KB and later infiltrate on the white square. White's plan is the exact opposite (exchange black-squared bishops and come in on the black squares). Look back at the Tarrasch-Teichmann ending (diagram 56). That arose from a French Defence in which White managed to trade black-squared bishops early in the game.

To look in some detail at the mechanics of a colour strategy in the opening/middlegame we shall turn our attention to the King's Indian Defence. Structurally speaking the K.I.D. is merely a French Defence seen through a mirror, but for some reason or other King's Indian strategy always seems more involved than its reflected counterpart. The following white-square strategy worked out by Petrosian is both subtle and illuminating: 1 P–Q4 N–KB3 2 P–QB4 P–KN3 3 N–QB3 B–N2 4 P–K4 P–Q3 5 B–K2 O–O 6 N–B3 P–K4 7 P–Q5.

Classically these closed K.I. positions lead to a race. White plays for P–QB5, Black counters with ...P–KB4 and may the best man win! Petrosian's idea is to manoeuvre for control of the white squares so as to take the sting out of Black's ...P–KB4 counter *before* launching his own queenside operations. After all the P–QB5 attack is inherent from the pawn structure and so will never disappear. Let us see how his idea operates by following a game Petrosian-Yuchtman:

7   ...   N–R3

If 7 ...N–K1 to play ...P–KB4 as quickly as possible, there comes 8 P–KR4 P–KB4 9 P–R5 opening the KR file against Black's castled king position. This is one reason for White closing the centre (7 P–Q5) before castling himself.

8   B–N5!

The key move. Superficially the motivation is obvious—Black cannot play ...P–KB4 without moving the knight and cannot move the knight without losing his queen—but the pin is easily broken. Under the surface lies the idea to weaken the white squares.

8   ...   P–KR3
9   B–R4   P–KN4

So what has been achieved? The bishop has been driven into oblivion and Black is now ready to move ...P–KB4 anyway. But he has made the vital concession ...P–KN4. As every Russian schoolboy knows, when you play ...P–KB4 and White replies KP×P, Black must recapture with the knight's pawn to prevent White gaining an outpost on K4. Now there is no knight's pawn with which to recapture—it has been drawn out of position in pursuit of the bishop. This means that ...P–KB4 can now never be played without presenting White with a beautiful outpost on K4.

10	B–N3	N–R4
11	N–Q2	N–B5

Securing an outpost for himself. White can never contemplate B×N in view of the reply ...KP×B! liberating the throttled bishop. White's whole strategy is to leave Black with a dummy bishop on N2.

11 ...N×B 12 RP×N P–KB4 would have played right into White's hands—13 P×P B×P 14 N(2)–K4 and 15 B–N4. White would later castle queenside and launch a direct mating attack based on the white squares and the KR file.

12	0–0	N–B4

Taking the other bishop would not help Black's cause either: 12 ...N×B+ 13 Q×N P–KB4 (13 ...N–B4 14 P–N4) 14 P×P B×P 15 N(2)–K4 and White can then start thinking in terms of QR–B1, P–QR3, P–QN4 and P–QB5, because there is no counterplay.

13	B–N4

The exchange of white-squared bishops is the next logical link in the chain of White's strategy.

13	...	P–QR4

Squandering his only chance which lay in 13 ...B×B 14 Q×B P–KR4! 15 Q–B5 P–R5, as pointed out by Petrosian. White is then forced to free Black's bishop from its self-captivity by 15 B×N KP×B and Black can later hold his damaged kingside together by ...Q–B3.

14	P–B3!

62

88   Black squares and white squares

Heralding the successful completion of White's opening strategy. He has completely disarmed Black's kingside, . . .P–KB4 being met by taking and following up with N(2)–K4, while the BN3 now has a cosy retreat to B2 in the event of . . .P–KR4–R5. He can now begin his queenside build-up with the utmost leisure. The race has been reduced to a one-horse affair—he only has to complete the course to win.

14 ... N(4)–Q6

An invasion into thin air, but there is no constructive plan to be found. If 14 . . .B×B 15 P×B White gets a super outpost for his knights on KB5.

15 Q–B2 P–QB3
16 K–R1 P–KR4
17 B×B R×B
18 P–QR3 P×P
19 BP×P N–B4

There is no way to maintain the knight on Q6, e.g. 19 . . .Q–Q2 20 B×N N×B 21 P–QR4 followed by P–QN3, N–B4, N–N5 etc.

20 B–B2 P–N5
21 P–KN3 N–N3

To put the other knight on Q6 would serve no useful purpose. Q6 is not a good outpost for Black—there is no pawn to support it. The very most a piece can hope for on such an isolated square is survival.

22 P×P P×P
23 B–K3

Still no hurry. Black's whole position is built on sand. He has white-square holes but no bishop to defend them, no capacity to expand or counter-attack. His present position may well be his optimal one, so give him some rope and . . .

23 ... P–QN4?

. . . he might sacrifice a pawn for nothing.

24 N×P Q–N3
25 P–QR4 Q–R3

Admitting the futility of his 23rd move. The rest is painful. 26 N–B4 P–B4 27 R×P R×R 28 P×R Q–N2 29 Q–N2 N–N6 30 N(5)×P Q–Q2 31 R–KB1 Black resigns.

There are essentially two types of white-square strategy. The first is as above: given a *fixed* pawn structure in which the enemy pawns are already on black squares, you exchange white-squared bishops with a view to setting up outposts or penetrating on white squares. The second is the same idea back to front: given a more fluid pawn set-up and that your opponent already has relinquished his white-squared bishop, you try to draw his pawns onto black squares. The objective is the same—to give the opponent a black-square pawn formation, but with no bishop to plug the gaps, but the build-up is different.

63

The position in diagram 63 arose from the opening of the game Stean-Planinc, Moscow 1975. There is as yet no question of bad bishops or weak squares. Indeed, neither player can reasonably claim to hold the advantage, though White's next move does set one or two problems.

1   N(R3)–B4

With threats to invade on N6 as well as the attack on the KP. Black can now maintain the balance with 1 ...N–Q2, but instead mistakenly resolves to eliminate the annoying knight.

1   ...   B×N?
2   B×B

2 N×B would leave the KP hanging, so why was Black's last move a mistake? Because his bishop on K3 was a good piece, too good to swap for a knight. If White can now find some way to lure the Black pawns onto black squares, he has all the makings of a successful white-square strategy.

2   ...   Q–Q2
3   P–KB3

To prevent the annoying ...N–N5 and also bolster the KP in preparation for B–N3 and N–B4.

3 ... N–R4
4 P–KN3

Keeping the knight out of KB5. There is no reason to fear 4 ...Q–R6 in view of 5 R–B2 followed by B–B1 and N–B4.

4 ... QR–Q1
5 B–N3!

64

So far White has been defending, but this move marks the turning of the tide. Black has reached the top of the hill and is about to roll all the way down again. Without his white-squared bishop he has no way of making any further impression on the white position, but instead must meet the threat of 6 N–B4 followed by B–N6 winning the QRP. The only way to do so involves the weakening of his white squares.

5 ... P–QB4
6 Q–K2

Of course not 6 B×P? Q×N. White can afford to take things very calmly. His domination of the white squares is probably already a winning advantage.

6 ... P–N3
7 KR–Q1 Q–B2
8 P–B3 N–B3

8 ...N–Q6? loses a piece to 9 N–B4.

9 N–B4 N–B3
10 N–R3

White has a number of good outposts for his pieces (all on white squares!). The knight has sniffed out one on QN5.

10	...	N–R2
11	Q–B4	KR–K1
12	K–N2	P–KR3

65

Having posted all his pieces (including his king) on good squares, White now has to tackle the problem of how to infiltrate. There is no obvious way to seize the open file, so he trades rooks to create more free space.

13	R×R	R×R
14	R–Q1	R×R
15	B×R	B–B1
16	B–K2	K–N2
17	Q–N3	N–K1
18	B–R6!	

The first hint of penetration. There is an immediate threat of 19 N–B4 winning the QNP (Black no longer has N–B1 as a defence), together with the long-term idea Q–Q5–R8 and B–N7 winning the knight on R2!

18	...	N–Q3
19	Q–Q5!	N–K1

He certainly cannot afford the further white-square weaknesses brought on by ...P–B3, e.g. 19 ...P–B3 20 N–B4 N(R2)–B1 (20 ...N×N 21 B×N and mates) 21 P–B4 P×P 22 B×P with winning threats.

20	N–B4	N–KB3

Losing a pawn, but he has no good defence anyway. This time 20
...P–B3 makes a spectacular exit viz. 21 N×NP! Q×N 22
B–QB4 22 ...Q×P+ 23 K–R3 with unstoppable mating threats.
Objectively best is 20 ...B–Q3, though he lacks a reply to 21
P–QN4! RP×P 22 P×P, e.g. 22 ...P×P 23 B×NP etc.

21 Q×KP and White won.

In conclusion, a warning to those who would willingly accept a
bad bishop and a few weak squares in return for the slightest
glimpse of an attack. As stressed earlier in the book, attacks must
be built on the basis of a definite superiority in your position,
either in development or in structure. To try to conjure up an
attack out of thin air by artificial means is simply asking for
trouble.

66

The position in diagram 66 is dead equal, however, in the game
Petrosian-Mecking, Palma 1969. Black (to move) allowed himself
to be carried away by dreams of an attack:

1   ...   B–N2

Normal would be 1 ...KR–Q1 with the bookmakers giving 3 to 1
on a draw.

2 B–B4   P–K4
3 B–QB1

Typical Petrosian. B–B4 was played with the sole intention of
provoking the reply ...P–K4. Mission accomplished, he has no
scruples about going back to square one. The bishop manoeuvre
has made two gains: (i) Black's KB is becoming 'bad'; (ii) an
outpost on Q5. Moreover the bishop retreat lures Black into a
false sense of optimism about his attacking chances.

Black squares and white squares   93

3	...	K–R1
4	B–Q5	

Exchanging off Black's better bishop.

4	...	B×B
5	P×B	P–B4

Black would be better advised to fix White's queenside on black squares by 5 ...P–QB5, but he is still dreaming of winning a great victory on the kingside.

6	P–QB4	QR–K1
7	R–Q1	P–B5?

Taking one step too many in the wrong direction. He must free his bishop with 7 ...P–K5 when Black's prospects are still not too bad, e.g. 8 P×P P×P 9 P–Q6 Q–B3 10 R–R7 B–Q5! 11 B–B4 with chances for both sides, though maybe a few more for White than for Black.

8	P×NP	QRP×P
9	Q–K4!	

67

Compare diagram 67 with diagram 66. White has made all kinds of positional gains: outpost on K4, good bishop *v.* bad bishop, protected passed pawn etc. And Black? He has been telegraphing his intention to deliver mate for some time, but has grossly underestimated his opponent's defensive possibilities.

9	...	Q–Q2
10	R–K1	

No need to panic. The secret of good defence is to keep calm and have faith in the inherent soundness of your position. In particular, don't be afraid of ghosts, i.e. don't make your opponent's threats out to be stronger than they actually are. For example, in this position Black has two dangerous-looking plans: (i) P–B6 and ...Q–R6; (ii) Q–R6 and ...R–B4–R4, but a simple calculation reveals them to be innocuous:

(i) 10 ...P–B6 11 R–R3 brings the attack to an immediate halt, as Black must defend his pawn.

(ii) 10 ...Q–R6 11 R–R3 R–B4 12 B×P! R–R4 13 Q–N2 and White has won a pawn for nothing.

10 ...   Q–KB2

Now trying his hand on the KB file, but again there is a simple defence.

11 R–K2

To meet ...P×P with RP×P and there is no way in.

11 ...   P–KN4
12 P–KN4!

Not only sealing up the kingside, but also fixing yet another pawn on a black square.

12 ...   Q–Q2

Or 12 ...P–B6 13 R–K1 P–R3 14 R–R3 and White can later round up the stray pawn.

13 P–B3

Completing his defensive programme. We now see the difference between strategy and attack. Attacks can be repulsed, but positional advantages do not suddenly vanish without trace. Petrosian's quiet but logical play has left him with a stranglehold on the white squares which he will be able to exploit now that Black's threats have dried up.

13 ...   R–R1
14 R×R   R×R
15 B–Q2

Stage one of the winning plan: tie Black's pieces to the defence of his KP.

15 ...   R–K1
16 B–B3   Q–Q3
17 R–K1

Stage two: switch to the QR file.

17 ...   P–R3

18	R–R1	R–KB1
19	R–R7	R–K1
20	Q–B5	

Stage three: penetrate on the white squares. It couldn't be simpler.

20	...	P–QN4

Or 20 ...R–KB1 21 Q–Q7 Q×Q 22 R×Q (threat R–K7) R–K1 23 R–N7 etc.

21	R–Q7	Q–B1
22	Q×Q+	R×Q
23	P×P	R–QN1?

A blunder in a hopeless situation.

24	R×B	Black resigns (24 ...K×R 25 B×P+)

7. Space

The essence of simple chess is mobility. Pieces need to be kept active and used economically. All the objectives of simple chess can be traced back to this underlying notion. Outposts are spring-boards from which pieces can generate activity, weak pawns hamper mobility because they require protection, 'bad' bishops are bad because their movements are restricted. However, the single most important factor in determining mobility must be space, but what is space? Terms like 'White has the freer game', 'White has greater control', 'Black is cramped', crop up frequently in annotations, but what do they really mean and how is space apportioned?

Unlike the ideas expressed so far in this book, space is not an easily definable or recognisable concept. The visual impression you obtain by glancing at a position and estimating who seems to have the lion's share can be misleading. The following is nearer the truth. Any given pawn structure has a certain capacity for accommodating pieces efficiently. Exceed this capacity and the pieces get in each other's way, and so reduce their mutual activity. This problem of overpopulation is easy to sense when playing a position—it 'feels' cramped. To take an example, compare diagrams 68 and 69.

68

They do, of course, represent the same position, but with two pairs of minor pieces less in the second case. In diagram 68 Black is terribly congested. There is no way he is ever going to be allowed to play ...P–QN4, while alternative methods of seeking some

breathing space by (after due preparation) ...P–K3 or
...P–KB4 would compromise his pawn structure considerably.
White on the other hand can build up at leisure for an eventual
P–K5, safe in the knowledge that so long as he avoids any piece
exchange, his adversary will never be able to free his game.
Diagram 69 is quite a contrast. The size of Black's forces is here
well within his position's 'capacity'. As a result there are no spatial
problems at all and Black can very quickly seize the initiative by
...P–QR3 and ...P–QN4 or even by ...P–QN4 as a pawn
sacrifice, e.g. 1 ...P–QN4 2 P×P P–QR3 3 P×P R×P with
tremendous pressure. We see from this pair of positions that
Black's structure is very good, but his capacity is small. Visually
White has a spatial advantage in both cases, but in the second the
eye flatters to deceive. In fact he is grossly overextended. A vast
empire requires an army of equal proportions to defend it.

Space is the most difficult element of chess strategy to understand. As we have just seen in diagram 68, a position can be
structurally very sound but actually very bad because of spatial
problems. The real test of our insight into the mechanics of an
advantage in space comes when confronted by a completely sound
(structurally), solid but cramped position. How do you exploit
such an advantage in space? Fischer provides all the answers.

70 White: R. J. Fischer, Black: F. Gheorghiu. Buenos Aires 1970

1 P–K4 P–K4 2 N–KB3 N–KB3 3 N×P P–Q3 4 N–KB3 N×P 5 P–Q4 B–K2 6 B–Q3 N–KB3 7 P–KR3 0–0 8 0–0 R–K1 9 P–B4 N–B3 10 N–B3 P–KR3

Black's position is very solid and devoid of weaknesses, yet he has some problems because his modest set-up is not equipped to hold a full complement of pieces. Put yourself in White's shoes and you might ask how you can possibly make any impression on the black position, but that is the wrong approach. For the time being White should maintain a low profile and concentrate on simple harmonious development, rather than which way he ought to be pointing his battering ram.

11 R–K1 B–B1

Naturally eager to swap off rooks.

12 R×R Q×R
13 B–B4 B–Q2
14 Q–Q2 Q–B1

There is no immediate danger, yet Black's position is uncomfortable. He wants to bring his rook to K1 but is unable to do so because his pieces are so constricted. For example, if 14 ...Q–K2 (to prepare ...R–K1), then 15 R–K1 and the queen must go back again. The only way to relieve the situation is by exchanges so Black prepares ...B–B4 to exchange bishops, thus liberating the Q2 square for his queen which in turn allows the rook a clear path to K1. For White's part it is sufficient to prevent this plan. When you have a spatial advantage there need be no hurry to form an active plan, that will come in due course. The important thing is to keep your opponent bottled up and put the onus on *him* to create active play. To do so he will be forced to weaken his own position somewhere. Only then do you pounce on him.

15 P–Q5

White would prefer to hold his pawns on Q4 and QB4, but this advance in conjunction with N–Q4 is the only way to prevent Black's freeing plan.

15 ...   N–N5
16 N–K4!

A neat finesse to preserve his KB and gain time for N–Q4, as the doubled pawns after 16 ...N×B 17 N×N+ are naturally unacceptable for Black.

16 ...   N×N
17 B×N   N–R3
18 N–Q4

71

Completing the hemming in manoeuvre. Now Black needs some fresh ideas. He can buy some space with 18 ...P–QB4, but this saddles him with some sick pawns after 19 P×P e.g. P×P. One of the main ideas in playing for space is that the opponent will some time 'trade off' his spatial inferiority for a structural one. Instead he elects to build an outpost on QB4 for his knight.

18 ...   N–B4
19 B–B2   P–QR4
20 R–K1   Q–Q1
21 R–K3!

The king's file is itself of no use to White because he has no entry point, but it does enable him to put his rook into active service on the third rank.

21 ...   P–QN3
22 R–KN3

White's greater command of space now transforms itself into a concrete attack. The justification for starting a direct offensive lies in the fact that Black's forces are concentrated on the queenside and are unable to transfer across to aid the defence.

22 ...   K–R1

The immediate threat was B×RP.

23 N–B3

Vacating the Q4 square for the queen. If Black seeks to anticipate this with 23 ...Q–B3, there comes 24 B–K3 and the bishop takes up the lease on Q4 with murderous effect.

23 ...   Q–K2
24 Q–Q4

72

The culmination of White's play. Black's kingside is raked by a crossfire of pins from which there is no shelter. Note that White is attacking with his entire army while Black is defending with but two pieces (queen and bishop), the rest being unable to communicate with the defence.

24 ...   Q–B3

The only defence to the threat of 25 B×RP (24 ...P–B3 25 N–R4 would be extremely gruesome).

25 Q×Q   P×Q

Now it's back to Chapter 3. The weakness of the shattered pawns is fatal. To begin with, White now has a juicy outpost on KB5.

26 N–Q4   R–K1

27 R–K3

Confident that his structural advantage is sufficient to win a minor piece ending. After 27 ...R×R 28 B×R K–N2 29 N–B5+ B×N 30 B×B the win is only a matter of time.

27 ... R–N1

Black shares his confidence. The remaining moves are desperation.

28 P–QN3 P–QN4
29 P×P B×NP
30 N–B5 B–Q2

He can if he prefers lose the pawn on R5 viz. 30 ...P–KR4 31 N–N3 P–KR5 32 N–B5.

31 N×RP R–N5
32 R–N3!

With two separate mating threats.

32 ... B×N
33 B×B N–K5
34 B–N7+ K–R2
35 P–B3 and Black resigns.

So we see how easy it can be (or rather seem to be) to squeeze an opponent to death without any recourse to violence. The strategy behind playing to exploit a space advantage is twofold:

(i) Deprive the opponent of any counterplay, avoiding exchanges whenever possible. The psychological pressure of being permanently hemmed in may well induce him to weaken himself in order to gain some freedom.

(ii) If no weaknesses are forthcoming you must be prepared to attack on *either* wing. Greater space control gives you better communication between flanks, so you naturally want to exploit this fact to build up against the adversary's weaker front. In our last game Fischer chose to attack on the kingside because of the sparsity of black forces in that region. Had the black pieces been concentrated on the kingside he would have resorted to a queen-side advance (P–QN4 and P–QB5). Flexibility of thought is needed to make use of flexibility on the board.

You have doubtless seen the move sequence 1 P–K4 P–K4 2 N–KB3 N–QB3 3 B–N5 P–QR3 4 B–R4 N–B3 5 0–0 B–K2 6 R–K1 P–QN4 7 B–N3 P–Q3 8 P–B3 0–0 9 P–KR3 N–QR4 10 B–B2 P–B4 11 P–Q4 Q–B2 12 QN–Q2 (diagram 73) leading to

the old main lines of the Ruy Lopez. Never in the history of chess have so many moves been repeated so often so quickly by so many people who didn't really understand them. Have you ever examined these well tried and trusted moves with a critical eye? Why, for example, should White spend twelve moves to develop just four pieces? Why waste four of these moves to preserve a bishop which will in all probability later become 'bad' when White blocks the centre with P–Q5 ? By answering these questions we can gain a lot of insight into White's overall strategy in the Lopez.

The first and most primitive idea behind 3 B–N5 is to lay siege to Black's KP which will subsequently be liquidated by P–Q4, thereby opening the floodgates for the white pawn centre to scatter the enemy forces with the allied pieces following up to rout the broken army—no prisoners taken. Black cannot however be forced to surrender the centre. By keeping his own KP firmly defended Black can thwart all White's aspirations of conquest in the centre, but this will lead to a rather cramped position. So the offspring of White's plan is an advantage in space due to the necessity for his opponent to maintain a firm central barricade. This spatial plus however is not very big and the only way to maintain it is by avoiding any exchange of pieces. Black's position (diagram 73) has sufficient 'capacity' for three minor pieces, but not clearly enough for all four of them. This explains why White is willing to invest so much time early in the game (B–N5–R4–N3–B2, P–KR3) purely to avoid exchanges. If his spatial strategy is to succeed he must leave Black with four minor pieces. These closed Ruy Lopez positions are some of the most subtle and complex in the whole opening repertoire. It is probably no coincidence that nearly all the great players of recent times have been deadly exponents of the Ruy Lopez. In the hands of Fischer or Karpov 3 B–N5 sometimes appears to win by force. For example, Karpov-Westerinen, Nice 1974. 1 P–K4 P–K4 2 N–KB3 N–QB3 3 B–N5 P–QR3 4 B–R4 P–Q3 5 0–0 B–Q2 6 P–Q4 N–B3 7 P–B3 B–K2 8 QN–Q2 0–0 9 R–K1 R–K1 10 N–B1 P–R3 11 N–N3 B–B1.

74

Here Black has adopted a less common form of defence. The idea is the same—to strongpoint his K4 pawn.

12   B–Q2

An unpretentious move, but White is not so much interested in promoting his own position as in containing his opponent's.

12	...	P–QN4
13	B–B2	N–QR4
14	P–N3	P–B4
15	P–Q5!	

75

This in conjunction with his last move keeps the knight on QR4 firmly out of play. If now 15 ...P–B5, then 16 P–N4 N–N2 17 P–QR4 gives White a clear structural advantage on the queenside because he can open the QR file at a time of *his* choosing, whereas Black can never resolve the position by ...P×P leaving himself with isolated pawns everywhere.

15 ...   N–R2
16 P–KR3

To meet ...N–N4 by N–R2 avoiding an exchange of knights.

16 ...   B–K2
17 N–B5

Confronting Black with a nasty dilemma. He needs to exchange some pieces to relieve his spatial problems, but ...B×N gives up his best minor piece. Were he to take the knight, he might well later fall victim to a white-square campaign, as his three central pawns all stand on black squares.

17 ...   N–N2

By bolstering the defence of his QP, Black now threatens to trade off his 'bad' bishop with ...B–N4.

18 P–QR4 P×P

He clearly has not seen White's reply or he would have continued according to plan 18 ...B–N4 19 N×B P×N.

19 P–QN4!

76

A surprise, but an entirely logical one. With this pawn thrust he keeps the black knight bottled up on N2 while laying down the foundations for a positive strategy. By recapturing on QR4 with his bishop White can start to get to work on the white squares. For example, he suddenly acquires an outpost on QB6. From the hazy depths of a purely spatial strategy we begin to see some concrete ideas emerging. It is very reasonable to assume that any position with an advantage in space will offer scope to translate the spatial plus into a structural one.

19 ... P–QR4

Black struggles hard to free himself by liquidating the queenside, but the idea of opening up the position is fraught with danger as the black pieces are much less mobile than their counterparts.

20 B×QRP RP×P
21 BP×P B–KB1

Changing plans in midstream is bound to be fatal, but so is the logical complement of Black's play 21 ...P×P on account of 22 B×B and now:

(i) 22 ...Q×B allows the bolt from the blue 23 N×KP!, as after 23 ...P×N 24 Q–N4 the double threat of mate and N×RP+ will cost Black his queen, while 23 ...R×R 24 Q–N4! R×R+ 25 B×R has similar effect.

(ii) 22 ...R×R 23 Q×R Q×B 24 B×QNP leaves Black powerless to prevent White's queen penetrating on the QR file, e.g. 24 ...Q–N4? 25 N×KP (again!) Q×B (or 25 ...P×N 26 N×B+) 26 N–B6 threatening mate on N7 as well as the queen and bishop.

22 B–B6!

Now Black is smothered. He cannot trade bishops because the knight on N2 would then have nowhere to go, so he must allow the establishment of a protected passed bishop in the midst of his queenside encampment.

22 ... Q–B2
23 P–N5 N–B3

Black's moves from this juncture are, essentially, irrelevant. There is no way he can in the long run hope to hold his queenside position, which has the look of Custer's last stand about it. Although he has only one vulnerable pawn (Q3), Black's pieces are so starved of space that they are themselves becoming targets of attack. After all, we only normally choose to attack pawns because of their inability to run away, but when the pieces themselves have no escape squares why not go in search of bigger game?

24 Q–B2 KR–N1

25	N–K3	B–B1
26	N–B4	B–K2
27	P–N6	Q–Q1
28	R–R7	

77

Making use of his latest acquisition, an outpost on R7! It is now only a matter of time before Black is pushed off the edge of the board.

28	...	N–Q2
29	Q–R4	R×R
30	P×R	R–R1
31	Q–R6	Q–B2
32	B×N(Q7)	

Winning by force. The entry of the white knight on QN6 is decisive.

| 32 | ... | Q×B |

Or 32 ...B×B 33 N–N6 winning at least a rook.

33	N–N6	N–Q1
34	Q–R1!	

Very artistic. If now 34 ...Q×P 35 Q×Q and 36 N×B, or 34 ...R×P 35 N×Q R×Q 36 R×R B×N 37 R–R7 winning some more, so Black resigned.

Undoubtedly the most difficult game in the book to understand. One can only really begin to appreciate the idea of converting spatial advantages into structural ones when the latter have been fully absorbed and understood. The closed Ruy Lopez positions represent a very fine balance between space and structure which only becomes apparent after many years of experience with them. When you understand the Lopez, you have mastered simple chess.

Our brief excursion into the Ruy Lopez has scratched the surface of some of the deeper aspects of chess strategy, but we will proceed no further in this direction. The idea of this book is to keep things simple, so let us look at some of the more direct consequences of spatial advantages. Space, or lack of it, is generally used as a way of persuading the opponent to make structural concessions. Let us take for example a (quite common) pawn structure, diagram 78.

78

Black's set-up is very sound but its 'capacity' is low, so given a position with some major pieces and a few minor pieces each, he would have some spatial problems. Structurally speaking he has two ways to combat them:

(i) Undermine White's centre by . . .P–QN4. This is the positionally correct method, but is in practice often difficult to organise as White can usually keep quite a strong grip on his QN5 square (with, say, knight on Q4, QB3, bishop on KB1–QR6 diagonal). An added problem is that moving the QNP gives White an outpost on QB6 for his knight.

(ii) Challenge White's pawn wedge by . . .P–K3. But this creates structural weaknesses. The black QP is left very weak after White exchanges pawns on K6 and the black kingside is also weakened somewhat.

Practice has shown that pawn structures akin to diagram 78 are very favourable for White providing that Black's minority attack . . .P–QN4 can be prevented. In this case the exploitation of

White's spatial advantage is not at all difficult to understand. He can utilise his greater control and communication between wings to launch a direct kingside attack.

79 White: L. Portisch, Black: S. Reshevsky. Petropolis 1973
1 P–QB4 P–QB4 2 N–KB3 P–KN3 3 P–K4 N–QB3 4 P–Q4 P×P 5 N×P N–B3 6 N–QB3 N×N 7 Q×N P–Q3 8 B–N5 B–N2 9 Q–Q2 0–0 10 B–Q3

We do not yet have the pawn structure of diagram 78, but White can some day plant his knight on Q5 and recapture with the KP when Black takes it off. Of course, the whole plan can be prevented by Black playing ...P–K3 at almost any stage, but this would leave him with a very sick QP on an open file. Simple chess always requires flexibility of thought. The opponent can always avert one form of weakness or disadvantage by accepting another somewhere else.

10 ...   P–QR4

Acknowledging from the start that he will never be permitted to play ...P–QN4, since after the natural plan of 10 ...R–N1 and 11 ...B–Q2 there comes P–QR4 by White and that's the end of that. Instead Black aims to steal some space on the queenside to offset his lack of it in the centre.

11 0–0   P–R5
12 QR–B1

To keep Black guessing. White could be intending to play N–Q5 and recapture with the bishop's pawn. You never can tell—

12 ...   B–K3
13 Q–B2

He can of course play N–Q5 immediately, as after 13 ...N×N 14 KP×N B–Q2 15 KR–K1 White stands better, but N–Q5 can never be prevented so why not probe a little first?

13 ... **N–Q2**

An indirect defence of the QRP (14 N×P? Q–R4 hitting two pieces). The natural 13 ...Q–R4 would make 14 N–Q5 correspondingly stronger:

(i) 14 ...N×N 15 KP×N and the Black KP is hanging.

(ii) 14 ...B×N 15 BP×B (you never could tell!) and White controls the QB file with an entry point on B7.

14 **P–B4**

A signal of the impending kingside attack. For the moment the threat is P–B5 winning the bishop.

14 ... **R–B1**
15 **P–QN3** **P×P**
16 **P×P** **N–B3**

Very passive, but alternatives are hardly more palatable:

(i) 16 ...N–B4 17 P–B5 N×B 18 Q×N B–Q2 19 N–Q5 leaves Black in terrible trouble (19 ...R–K1 20 P–B6!).

(ii) 16 ...P–B4 17 QR–K1 and the pressure on the king's file is felt right the way back to Black's KP.

17 **K–R1** **Q–R4**
18 **P–B5** **B–Q2**
19 **N–Q5!**

80

The moment we've all been waiting for. After 19 ...N×N 20 KP×N, White has through his spatial advantage very good attacking chances against the black king, e.g. 20 ...KR–K1 21 QR–K1 Q–Q1 22 P×P RP×P 23 B×NP! P×B 24 Q×P R–B1 25 B–R6 forcing mate.

19 ... Q–Q1!

A good defensive try, in that 20 N×N+ B×N 21 B×B P×B leads nowhere for White as he is left with a bad bishop and many black-square weaknesses. The correct way to pursue the attack is by increasing the pressure without permitting too much simplification.

20 Q–B2 B–B3
21 Q–R4 B×N

The presence of the knight on Q5 has eventually proved too much for Black to tolerate, but now White obtains the pawn formation he has been seeking all along.

22 KP×B R–K1
23 R–KB3 N–Q2
24 QR–KB1 B–B3

Black would like to establish his knight on the outpost at K4, but then there would come 25 R–R3 P–R4 26 P×P P×P 27 B×NP! N×B 28 Q×P N–B1 29 Q–B7 mate. Instead he hopes to trade bishops and erect a defence on the black squares, but in doing so he is destroyed by a combination.

25 R–R3 N–B1
26 P×P BP×P
27 B×NP! P×B
28 R×B!

and Black resigned as it is mate after 28 ...P×R 29 Q–R8+ K–B2 30 R–R7+ N×R 31 Q×N+ K–B1 32 B–R6.

Another game in which correct nursing of a spatial plus results in a direct attack:

81 White: V. Smyslov, Black: K. Gudmundsson. Reykjavik 1974
1 P–Q4 N–KB3 2 N–KB3 P–KN3 3 P–QN3 B–N2 4 B–N2 0–0 5 P–N3 P–Q3 6 B–N2 P–B4 7 0–0 N–B3 8 P–Q5 N–QR4 9 P–B4 P–QR3 10 QN–Q2 P–QN4 11 P–K4 R–N1 12 B–B3 Q–B2 13 P–K5 N–N5 14 KP×P KP×P 15 B×B K×B

It is immediately obvious that White has more space because of his pawn wedge on Q5, but Black has obtained an aggressive set-up on the queenside by ...P–QN4. Indeed, one might even venture to say that Black has a slight structural superiority because he has some pressure on the base of White's pawn centre (QB4) and first option on the QN file, whereas the counter-pressure against the base of Black's centre (Q3) is not evident. Once again the trouble with Black's position is with com-munications. His queenside position is a favourable one, but lacks contact with the rest of the war effort. If White can successfully conduct a holding operation on the queenside, some of Black's pieces (particularly the NQR4) will be left very much out of play.

16 R–K1   P–B3

To increase the pressure on White's QBP by establishing a knight on K4. In the event of an exchange there, Black wants to recapture with the KBP. The immediate 16 ...N–K4 17 N×N P×N not only gives his adversary a strong passed pawn, but also weakens his own QBP, e.g. 18 R–QB1 threatening 19 P×P P×P 20 P–QN4!

17 Q–B1

Sounder than Q–B2 which might some time allow an embar-rassing ...B–B4. Besides, with his central pawn configuration on white squares he would prefer his queen on a black square as a matter of principle.

17 ...   N–K4
18 B–B1

Completing his consolidation of the queenside. For the moment White's position looks to be the more passive, as indeed it is. But at this point the spatial considerations begin to take over. Black's position has already almost reached its peak. He has no capacity to expand or exert more pressure without creating weaknesses in his own camp. On the other hand, the White forces although temporarily at a low ebb, have plenty of opportunity to drive forward in the longer term because of the greater space poten-tially available to them.

18 ...   B–N5

In essence the right idea—Black would like to force some exchanges—but his mission turns out to be singularly unsuc-cessful. He would do better to trade knights while he still has the chance, e.g. 18 ...N×N+ 19 N×N P×P 20 P×P R–N5 possibly followed by the manoeuvre N–N2–Q1–B2–K4. Black is willing to expend a great deal of time and energy to provoke the exchange of the second pair of knights. His position is fundamentally quite sound, but simply lacking in space.

19 N–R4!

Very instructive. White wants to avoid exchanges, so any old square will do for the knight as long as all the pieces stay on.

19 ...   P×P
20 P×P   KR–K1
21 P–B4

The great wheel of fortune begins to turn in White's favour. As he expands his own position the black pieces will start to tread on each other's toes for lack of space.

21 ...   N–B2

Q2 would be a better square for the knight, but this would excommunicate the bishop (22 P–KR3 etc.).

22 Q–B3

The threat to win a pawn by 23 N–K4 Q–Q1 24 N×KBP Q×N 25 Q×N now induces a full-scale retreat.

22 ...   R×R
23 R×R   N–N2
24 P–KR3   B–Q2
25 N–K4   Q–Q1
26 P–N4!

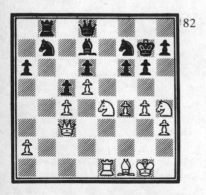

82

Compare this with White's modest position some ten moves ago. His conquest of space has brought him a decisive kingside attack (the threat of P–N5 is unstoppable) almost as an incidental by-product.

26 ...   P–KR3
27 B–Q3

Smyslov chooses the most elegant method. Naturally the cruder 27 P–N5 is also very strong.

27 ...   P–N4
28 N–N3!

The point of his previous move. White can give up a piece for a mating attack. The subsequent helplessness of the Black forces is quite remarkable.

28 ...   P×N
29 N–R5+ K–B1
30 N×P   B–R5

What else? There is nothing to be done against 31 N–R5 and 32 Q–N7 mate.

31 N–R5   N–K4
32 P×N and Black resigned.

Playing on the basis of a spatial advantage is in a sense a question of blind faith. You see no targets in the enemy position and no way to force any weaknesses, but merely attempt to fortify your own position allowing simplification only when absolutely necessary or clearly favourable in the belief that your opponent will some time feel obliged to make concrete concessions in terms of pawn weaknesses or outposts in order to avoid suffocation. The difficult part of a spatial strategy lies not in the execution which is relatively simple, but in the recognition of the fact that you actually do have an advantage in space. As already mentioned, the vital criterion is not necessarily whether you 'appear' to control more of the board. This is undoubtedly a yardstick, but not always an accurate one. The real criterion is whether your opponent has more pieces than can comfortably fit in with his pawn structure, and this you can only really expect to assess correctly on the basis of experience. From your own games and by studying master games you can gradually acquire a feeling for the 'capacity' (as I earlier termed it) of certain pawn structures. Space is not an easy concept to define with precision or understand with clarity, but time and practice will sharpen your awareness of it as a factor in chess. I have tried throughout the book to lay down principles and put forward ideas that relate to all phases of the game, opening, middlegame and endgame, and space is no exception. The role played by space in the endgame is in fact much more straightforward than in the middlegame. In endings the king assumes great power and, consequently, value. The advantage of being first to occupy the centre with your king is considerable. He who commands more space has more squares for his king, it's as simple as that. More space means a potentially stronger king.

83 White: T. Petrosian, Black: L. Portisch. 5th game Candidates' Match 1974

1 P–QB4 N–KB3 2 N–KB3 P–QN3 3 P–KN3 P–QB4 4 B–N2 B–N2 5 0–0 P–K3 6 N–B3 B–K2 7 P–Q4 P×P 8 Q×P 0–0 9 R–Q1 N–B3 10 Q–B4 Q–N1 11 P–K4 Q×Q 12 B×Q KR–Q1 13 P–K5 N–K1 14 N–Q4 N–R4 15 P–N3 B×B 16 K×B P–KN4 17 B–K3 K–N2

White has more space on account of his advanced pawn on K5 which in turn gives him a very good square on K4 for his king, while Black through lack of space has no central squares available for his own leader.

18 P–B4

A surprising move in that White voluntarily places his pawns on squares of the same colour as his bishop, but Petrosian reckons his grip on the centre to be more important.

18 ... P×P
19 P×P N–QB3
20 N(B3)–K2

Against the natural 20 K–B3 there comes 20 ...P–B4 barring the white king from K4, but now 20 ...P–B4 can be met by 21 N×N P×N 22 N–Q4 winning a pawn.

20 ... N×N
21 N×N B–B4

Continuing with his policy of exchanges. If 21 ...QR–B1 White has the strong continuation 22 N–N5 P–QR3 23 B×P!

P×N 24 B×R R×B 25 P×P netting a rook and an impressive array of passed pawns for two pieces.

22 K–B3 P–Q3
23 R–Q2!

A remarkably strong move after which the black king suddenly finds himself in trouble. He could of course abdicate his responsibilities and seek refuge on some godforsaken edge of the board where he would be relatively safe, but then the rest of the position would crumble through lack of his support. For example, White threatens QR–Q1 followed by N–N5 with decisive threats on the queen's file. Black's only chance of survival is to bring his king into the centre to bolster his defences.

23 ... P×P
24 P×P B×N

Again Portisch seeks to relieve his position by exchanges, but this still does not help his king to find a satisfactory square in the centre.

25 B×B P–B3

Desperation, but if 25 ...K–B1, then 26 QR–Q1 leaves Black defenceless viz.

(i) 26 ...K–K2 27 P–B5 QR–N1 (27 ...P–N4 28 P–B6!) 28 P×P P×P 29 B×P! R×R 30 B–B5+.

(ii) 26 ...N–N2 (or B2) 27 B×P! R×R 28 B–B5+.

(iii) 26 ...R(Q1)–B1 27 B–K3 followed by B–R6+ etc.

26 P×P+ N×P
27 R–KB1!

Threatening to win a piece by 28 K–K3.

27 ... K–R3
28 R–K1

Winning the KP as 28 ...R–K1 unpins the bishop allowing 29 B×N, while 28 ...R–Q3 loses to 29 B–K3+. The rest is very one-sided: 28 ...N–N1 29 R×P+ K–R4 30 R–K5+ K–N3 31 R–N2+ K–B2 32 R–K4 N–B3 33 R–B4 R–Q3 34 R–N5 QR–Q1 35 R–Q5! Black resigns (35 ...R×R 36 R×B+ K–K2 37 P×R).